THE GALACTIC SUN DEAD ONE #0115

Brett Lewis Blatherwick

THE GALACTIC SUN DEAD ONE #0115

Vanguard Press

VANGUARD PAPERBACK

© Copyright 2024
Brett Lewis Blatherwick

The right of Brett Lewis Blatherwick to be identified as author of
this work has been asserted by him in accordance with the
Copyright, Designs and Patents Act 1988.

All Rights Reserved

No reproduction, copy or transmission of this publication
may be made without written permission.
No paragraph of this publication may be reproduced,
copied or transmitted save with the written permission of the
publisher, or in accordance with the provisions
of the Copyright Act 1956 (as amended).

Any person who commits any unauthorised act in relation to this
publication may be liable to criminal prosecution and civil claims for
damages.

A CIP catalogue record for this title is available from the British
Library.

ISBN 978-1-80016-854-1

This is a work of fiction. Names, characters, businesses, places, events and
incidents are either the products of the author's imagination or are used in a
fictitious manner. Any resemblance to actual persons, living or dead, or actual
events is purely coincidental.

Vanguard Press is an imprint of
Pegasus Elliot Mackenzie Publishers Ltd.
www.pegasuspublishers.com

First Published in 2024

Vanguard Press
Sheraton House Castle Park
Cambridge England

Printed & Bound in Great Britain

If you get assigned to the fryolator one more time, you are going to lose it. You hate your manager, and you hate working at Burger Hut, but most of all you hate the smell of French fries cooking in a rancid vat of oil. You clock in, tie on an apron, and – surprise, surprise – Ken has you on fry duty again. Jerk. You go into the walk-in freezer to grab a bag of frozen fries, but when you turn around, the freezer is gone. In fact, the entire Burger Hut is gone. So is the year 2020! You discover that you are on a potato farm in rural Ireland in 1545. You don't know what to do, until it dawns on you that no one here knows how to make a French fry. With your advanced knowledge on the subject, you could make a ton of money and become a lord or something. You knock on the potato farmer's door, introduce yourself, and discuss your business plan. After a minute, he slams the door in your face. You begin to lose hope, but when the farmer's beautiful daughter approaches you and expresses her interest in your food invention, you think you have found your business partner – and perhaps something much more.

A disease has wiped out most of the inhabitants of a colonized planet. You are the only surviving geneticist, and it's up to you to create a genetically modified, disease-resistant human hybrid to save the population. You venture into the vast alien wilderness to find a solution before it's too late.

In the near future, genetically-modified locusts who have been designed to swarm continuously escape a laboratory and ravage farmlands across the Earth. The world is slowly dying, but you find a way to survive by growing crops indoors with plant-growing lamps and solar panels. The windows and doors of your house are boarded up, but you can still hear the swarm outside as they try to find a way into your home to eat what is left of the world's vegetation.

Intergalactic space travel has become commonplace, with people across various solar systems working together to form new governments and societies. An astronaut falls in love with a beautiful alien from another planet. Unfortunately, from her species' perspective, humans are viewed as being quite hideous. He goes about trying to impress her with limited success, and hijinks ensue.

Since the beginning of time, alien civilizations have experienced three phases of societal evolution. During the first phase, society procures resources from its own planet. The second phase occurs when planetary resources are exhausted and society must travel through space to gather additional resources. The third phase arises when space travel becomes an insufficient method for procuring resources, and time travel is then invented and used to acquire resources throughout history. As one of the most resource-abundant planets in the galaxy, Earth begins to garner attention from other species who are within their second or third phases. Humanity must steal technological advancements from these alien civilizations and develop a planetary space force capable of time travel to protect what is rightfully theirs.

You have been chosen to become an oracle in ancient Greece. Your mother and her mother before her were oracles as well, consulting the gods and relaying their wishes to heroes and others across the years. But there is one problem: you have never heard a word from the gods. Regardless, you pretend you do, and the next couple of weeks go relatively smoothly, although you do feel guilty for giving false advice to those few unlucky heroes. But when a kind young woman in a hooded cloak arrives, seeking guidance from you specifically, you confess. You tell her not to heed your advice, for you cannot commune with the gods. You beg her not to tell anyone else. She smiles, removing her hood. Something inside of you tells you that this is the Goddess Athena. You fall to your knees, and she shakes her head, thanking you for your honesty. She requests you come with her. In shock, you agree, and, with a simple touch of her hand, you are transported to the halls of Olympus, where you train with Athena and learn that the names of each god are titles passed down through many people. You are to become the next one.

When you wake up one morning to find that your wife has aged by fifty years, you wonder if you had one too many tequila shots the night before. Your geriatric wife manages to tell you she is not from this time, but a traveler from the past who has been trapped here for years. As a result of this, the aging process of her body isn't working properly, and she needs to return to her own time to survive. The problem is, her rapidly deteriorating memory means she can't remember where she hid the device that allows her to travel in time.

You're not a fan of time travel. It's expensive, it's dangerous, and the regulations don't allow you to alter the timeline anyway, so why bother? Besides, you spend your days and most of your nights working on the tech to keep the machines running, which doesn't leave you with much spare time. But one day, as you're fixing a minor issue in the data mainframe, a woman comes storming in with a gun and demands you go with her – to 1854. She takes your key card, which is the only way to activate the machine, and off you go. You don't know anything about that time period, but you don't have a choice in the matter. Yet the further the adventure goes and the longer you're with her, the more intrigued you become. This woman is on a mission and, as mysterious as she is, you find that you can't help but believe her. You're also starting to think there's more between you than just happenstance – that she chose you for a reason.

An alien spacecraft has landed but looks like a living, breathing organism. It sits for a while as Earth's scientists observe it, and they find that the entire ship is a biomechanical life-form of gigantic proportions. With vein-like structures mixing with wires, and a core generator that pumps liquid like a heart, the vessel remains quiet except for its breath-like hissing. You are part of a team of scientists tasked with entering the vessel's main door, which looks frighteningly like a mouth.

You are on an expedition to find a planet that humans can colonize. Rule number one is to not engage with any sentient life. You never thought it would be an issue; after all, living beings are rare on new planets. However, the planet you're sent to investigate is home to various creatures, many of whom are highly intelligent. When you're attacked by locals after an excursion for wildlife goes wrong, one alien risks everything to save you from his people. You never meant to disobey your orders. It was a situation you could not avoid. However, you don't think your superiors will understand if you fall in love with this alien. It is a temptation that is hard to resist.

You've been mapping the galaxy for thirty years, during which time you've made contact with two alien races, but you've never seen a planet like this. All the necessities of life are there: water, air, plant abundance, and stability. But there are no animals. Your crew has been taking readings for hours, and they have found nothing. Your crew grows more comfortable, spreading out across the landing site and into the forests, valleys, and meadows. The cloud comes suddenly, descending from the mountains without warning. You've been doing this long enough to know you should be afraid, and you race back to the ship in time, along with a few lucky souls. Others aren't so quick. The bugs coat the land like the air itself, one massive unending mantle of buzzing, whirring blackness. Most of your men die instantly. The insects are so thick they are clogging the exhaust ports of the ship and even swarming their way into the thruster engines. When you receive a broken radio transmission from some of your men who have somehow survived the swarm for now, you must decide if you should wait out the insects or try to save your men.

Your colonial planet is an outlier in the galaxy, but extremely famous, as it is the only place Whisperlings are known to natively inhabit. The creatures have developed biopigmentation control, which allows them to change color to match their surroundings, making them invisible when motionless and nearly so when moving. They're also impervious to the electrotraps commonly used to catch prey on the planet. The beasts are incredibly difficult to find and are fearsome fighters, but hunting them is the highest honor. It is believed that their DNA may contain the secret to invisibility, as well as a host of other genetic engineering mysteries. Today is your test. You and your fellow village boys are each given a tiny hoverboard, a single spear, and enough food and water to last a day. You are to catch the largest prey you can and return as soon as possible, and your results – both speed of the catch and size of the prey – will be compared with those of the other boys.

You and your husband are inventors who finally discover the secret to time travel. You agree that this year's vacation will be to New York in the 1960s. Unfortunately, something goes terribly wrong, and you both end up in separate eras, lost in time. How will you find your way back to one another?

You're one of the last surviving humans on Earth. Most others abandoned the planet soon after the final world war. After five long years of not seeing another person, you stumble upon an alien spacecraft. You try to run away, but are captured and brought back to the ship. When the mysterious alien leader sees that you're sick and alone, he takes you under his protection. You fight against it at first, but eventually realize that his intentions are pure. The more time you spend together, the more you come to respect him and his alien nation. Although it doesn't make sense, at least not at first, you feel something a bit more than respect: you start to fall in love.

Six months ago, a single alien spaceship encountered Earth and started a war that obliterated half of humanity. The surviving nations have united in their desperation and are holding on by their fingertips. The aliens, meanwhile, are attempting to contact their home planet and request an invasion force to finish the job that they started. You don't know yet exactly how much time is needed to send the signal, but you do know that if the aliens are able to communicate with their home world, it would mean the end of life as we know it. Humanity has only one chance of survival: destroy the alien ship before the signal is sent. The surviving nuclearized powers have banded together and confirmed that they have enough firepower to completely destroy the alien ship that started the war. However, the ship's shields must be down for the plan to have any chance of success. You are the leader of a special ops team tasked to infiltrate the alien ship, sabotage its shields, and escape before the nuclear missiles hit their target.

Immortality treatments mean that people like you have legal records that go back centuries, even for petty crimes. As the world becomes more crowded, your life on Earth is severely restricted because of a handful of bad decisions in your youth. A company is seeking volunteers to travel thirty light-years away to colonize a new planet, where people could have the opportunity for a fresh start – with the understanding that there may be intelligent life-forms there that need to be defeated. You sign up for the journey.

Earth has become uninhabitable and you're tasked with finding a new planet where humans can live. In the search, you come across a planet inhabited by beings who are half animal/half man, and have set up societies much like packs of animals do, with alpha leaders and pack-hunting traits.

You are an advanced alien life-form sent on a special mission to Earth to exterminate all humans, who have repeatedly demonstrated their negative effect on space. When your pod malfunctions and crashes, a kind human woman saves you. Now, you are conflicted between the love you feel for her and your mission to destroy her race.

Your life was uneventful until New Year's Eve, 2019, when a strange portal opened in the air in front of you and a panicked figure ran out, claiming to be from the future.

She said she wanted to save you from government agents from her time, who were about to travel here to kill you. She explained that, some time in the future, you will create a technology rendering all other energy sources useless. You laughed, telling her you were a broke college student who eats ramen three times a day. Before you could convince her she had the wrong person, another portal materialized.

An airborne virus released in 1989 by the Russians during the Soviet–Afghan War infects millions of people worldwide, turning them into winged gargoyle creatures. Modern technology is wiped out. As one of the unaffected humans, you must hunt the infected humans if you are to survive.

After the American military discovered a crashed alien vessel containing a genetically advanced life-form, they used its genome to create an army of humanoid super-soldiers able to withstand significant pain and physical damage before dying. Little do they know that it was a trap, and they have unintentionally created a sleeper cell of humanoid beings with allegiance to an alien planet. One day, that sleeper cell is activated – and it is your job to stop them.

Millions of years have passed, and the planet has become hostile to human life. Starvation has killed off most of the world's human population and infertility has ensured no more will be born. The last few survivors now face extinction as new wild predators force humanity down the food chain. You are one of these survivors, hoping to find a settlement that can withstand Earth's inhospitable environment.

Your dog-walking business in New York City has been doing well for the past few years. You work mostly with wealthy clients who have nine-to-five office jobs, and you have walked everything from Pomeranians to Great Danes. When one client sends for you via handwritten letter, your interest is piqued. You reread the letter and find a P.S. on the back regarding some sort of charm that the dog must wear to conceal his appearance. You disregard the odd statement and decide to visit the address listed. The next day, you find yourself at the door of a penthouse in an old art deco apartment building. Having read that the dog is fussy and bites, you have brought along your gardening gloves to protect your hands. But as you unlock the door with the key the client left for you under the mat, you find that what she wants you to walk isn't your typical dog. It's Cerberus, the guardian hound of the underworld. You're definitely going to need more than gardening gloves.

To extend their life-spans, humans have created an elixir that can cure most diseases. The main ingredient for this medicine can be found only on a few planets. Therefore, to acquire this ingredient, humanity has developed a massive galactic military whose sole mission is to conquer worlds which have this particular resource. During humanity's latest attempt to subjugate a world, Earth's forces have encountered pushback from the native inhabitants of the planet. You are one of these aliens, battling a technologically-advanced human species. However, when you discover that the elixir has narcotic properties and that your foes cannot function without it, you believe that you have found your enemy's Achilles' heel.

You are a member of an alien race that has been exploring space for over a millennium, seeking out other life-forms and establishing alliances with them. During one of your missions, you discover Earth on long-range scanners and decide to investigate. You and your team are excited to find sentient life-forms on the planet, and you begin observing them from afar. Then, out of nowhere, your ship is suddenly confronted with military spacecraft, with guns aimed at you.

You climb off the city water-taxi wearing your favorite summer dress. You look around and spot your best friend at your usual picnic spot in Marina Park. As you pay your fare, someone bumps your shoulder, causing you to drop your handbag. You pick it up, glancing back in surprise to the woman you've had your eye on in AP Bio all semester. She's tall, blonde, slender, pale, and exactly your type. You've wanted to get to know her better, but you were too shy to introduce yourself. You look away. She seems busy tuning her guitar anyway. You walk in the other direction and finally join your friend. As you sit down and start talking, you can hear your crush in the background as she plays her guitar. A few people come by and drop money into her hat as she strums a tune and sings. She's incredibly good – singing, dancing, and playing her guitar as you watch her from the corner of your eye – and you are having a hard time ignoring her as you try to catch up with your friend. Noticing how distracted you are, your best friend decides to play matchmaker and drags you closer to the singer. "Come on! Maybe you can drop your phone number in her hat instead of money? I think she would appreciate it more!"

You begrudgingly follow your friend. When you get there, you spot an enormous man with a serpent tattoo on his shoulder, watching with a scowl on his face. Wait. Did the serpent tail on his tattoo just move? As the blonde finishes her set, she catches your eye and smiles at you. Before you can react, the big man rushes forward and grabs the singer. In a thick Bulgarian accent, he yells, "Samodiva! This is for my sister!"

The crowd screams and fans out. After the scuffle is over, the man runs off, leaving the singer on the ground. Someone in the crowd calls the police as you hurry to her side. She asks you to get her out of there. Her hand is clutching at her stomach, where a silvery ooze is visible. Is that her blood? She locks eyes with you again, this time with a plea. "Don't say a word." You nod. Whatever is going on, for some reason you trust her, and you're determined to save her.

You and your mother work hard every day to keep your grain farm running in the height of the Great Depression. You feel connected to the land in a way you can't explain, and your mother is a genius at knowing just how to make the crops flourish. Beyond this great closeness to the land, your bond with your mother is unshakable. Life is peaceful and tough, but fulfilling. The only thing missing for you is romance, but you believe that, when it's time, it will come to you. One night, you wake to see a purple orb glowing in the fields. A powerful force compels you to get out of bed and go to it. It's the dead of night, but you can't help yourself. When you get there, you find a hooded man holding a long staff, with the light that led you there emanating from the top of the staff. You don't run or scream, but you can't understand why. Then he greets you by your name: Persephone. He tells you his master would like to meet you. He waves the staff and, to your shock, the ground opens beneath your feet, but you do not fall. Instead, you see a stunning gentleman on a chariot tied to a pair of majestic horses beneath your feet. He asks you to join him for a ride. Before you can reply, your mother's scream rips through the night.

A thousand years ago, a rapidly progressing Ice Age forced humanity to abandon Earth. Ten massive ships carrying millions of people were launched into space to escape the devastation and have orbited the frozen planet ever since. Over the years, these ships have become nations unto themselves, developing separate militaries and engaging in wars with one another. As another conflict brews between two ship-nations, you receive a faint radio signal from the Earth's surface. You decide to investigate it further, despite the orders of your superior officer.

The creatures first arrived in globes of glass, dropped from the invaders' spaceships like a hailstorm of massive bubbles. When they struck the ground they shattered, releasing the bugs into the world. The aliens sent a message with this biological weapon, saying that human beings will eventually devour one another. The first symptoms of this biological weapon are hallucinations that involve visions of your friends and family. In the visions, they mock you, beat you, or kill themselves. Whatever most people naturally find harmful, the parasite inputs those precise experiences into their brains. The bugs seem an impossible quirk of evolution or an incarnation of hell. They feed specifically on chemicals released during fearful, life-threatening, or painful situations. They are frighteningly advanced. They land on the nape of the neck and burrow into the spinal column, absorbing the host's impulses until they've learned enough to input illusions of their own making. They quickly take control, convincing the host it is facing a living hell and feeding until the host is drained dry. When your family dies, you are staunchly determined to find an uninfected island where you can live in peace.

A planet has been discovered that contains vast resources located underneath its surface. A group of experienced miners and a battalion of Earth's military are sent to the desolate planet to obtain these resources. As the miners drill down into the planet's crust, they encounter strange alien creatures who will defend their underground world at any cost. You are a member of the space troopers ordered to defend the miners and you must find a way to fight these aliens before all is lost.

During a war in the Middle East, one side decides to unleash its latest weapon: a deadly mutagenic virus that can directly damage the genome of a person. After being deployed on the battlefield, the virus quickly spreads throughout the world. Those who survive the infection become horrendously deformed and mentally unstable, mindlessly roaming from place to place and attacking anything or anyone that can be consumed. As an astronaut on the international space station, you and your team watch from afar as the city lights that once covered the Earth slowly go out one by one. After a month, you receive a radio signal from an underground bunker saying that they have discovered a cure. With your supplies running out, you and your fellow astronauts have little choice but to return home.

Upon discovering a planet that seems remarkably similar to Earth, you decide to take a landing party down to explore it. The first day passes smoothly. The planet seems to be a miracle, a paradise of plenty. Then night comes, and an odd smell emerges. You feel faint and soon black out. When you awake, your crew is gone, while men and creatures are rushing toward you through the darkness, shrieking for blood. You turn to run, but a woman's screams draw your attention. You are stunned to see Nialla, an old love, running down the slope, pursued by a gang wearing Kashari smuggler masks. You rush toward her, shooting at the smugglers, only to find they aren't Kashari at all. They are your family. Enduring several minutes of hell and horror, you eventually realize these are nothing but illusions built from your own memories. Something in the air is causing hallucinations that seem freakishly real. You are left to find your crew in the middle of a living nightmare, hoping this is a mere natural phenomenon and not some sinister alien technology turned upon you.

You live in a lunar colony in which genetic modification has reached a tipping point. Large corporations have moved past using A.I. to replace human workers and have begun to sell genetically modified 'workers', enslaved and auctioned to the highest bidder. These workers are modified to be excellent at their particular job. You fall in love with one of these modified beings and set your mind to rescue her.

A vast empire is expanding across the galaxy, continually colonizing habitable planets. You are the captain of an explorer vessel seeking ways to increase the size and strength of the empire. The most recent discovery is a planet full of valuable resources, but its princess begs you to leave her planet alone. You fall in love with her, but can't hide your discoveries from your superiors.

You are part of a military reconnaissance team tasked with surveying a newly discovered planet and determining whether it is an ideal location for a base. While on the ground, your team encounters a vicious creature which no one has ever seen before. At first, your team thinks that these creatures are typical pack animals and ignores them for the most part, except for the occasional target practice. However, when you analyze their attack behavior and find out that they understand military tactics, you realize that they are not as wild as they seem. The next night, when the lights go out at your campsite and you see their glowing red eyes from the nearby forest, you know you are in for the fight of your life.

A handsome stranger moves to your small town, and all the single women are desperate to impress him. As a shy bookworm, you spend your time working at the local library and reading the classics. You are surprised when the newcomer frequents the library daily, reading old journals. The two of you bond over your love of books, and there is something different about him that makes you fall for him. One day after he leaves, you chance upon one of the books he has been reading, which details the town's history. You are shocked when you look at a picture of the town's founders and see someone who looks identical to the newcomer.

You are desperate for money to pay your rent, so you sign up to take part in a clinical trial, despite it being a little vague on the details. You're not complaining because the money is great! But when they strap you to a machine with a dozen different wires, you start to worry. It's too late to back out now. After a flash, the room fades. You wake up in an alleyway, confused and disoriented. When a car flies overhead, you know something has gone wrong. Somehow, you have ended up in the future. Panicked, you find the nearest floating police station, but the officers laugh you out. One of the officers believes your story and offers to help you. As the two of you grow closer while trying to unravel the mystery of what happened to you, your feelings for her grow, too.

Life in the Scottish Highlands in the early 1600s isn't always easy. Luckily, you work for a good laird, who is always kind and considerate to his workers. Although the kitchen is hot and the work is tiring, you are happy with your life. But one night, as you're readying for bed, a strange man appears out of nowhere. He tells you that there will be a fire and he is here to save you. He grabs your hand and before you can say anything, you're somewhere new. He tells you that you're in the twenty-first century. You call him a liar, a witch, but he explains that he is a time traveler who has brought you to his time to protect you. You don't believe him, but you also don't know how to explain what you are seeing around you. You bide your time to survive, all the while learning that there's more than meets the eye with the handsome, mysterious captor.

You're just enjoying your day off from work, thinking about maybe watching that new movie that people keep talking about, when the literal air splits around you and a man appears out of nowhere. He's tall and handsome, and he tells you that he's been sent from the future to protect you. You think he's crazy – except you did see him come from nowhere. When he grabs your hand, you feel a spark. This man is here to save your life – and change it forever.

You've been lost for nearly as long as you can remember – jumping from year to year, from time to time. You never stay for long, and you cannot control when or where you land. One day, after being thrown from ancient

Greece to the Roaring Twenties in America, you find yourself stuck. You're unsure what's changed or how long this reprieve will last. Then, you meet him. He's handsome and charming. Weeks turn into months. He tells you that he loves you, and you realize that, for the first time, you are in love. This must be why you've been lost in time: you were looking for him all along. You tell him as much. You fall asleep in his arms. When you wake up, you are in Russia in 1670. You don't know how, but you know you must make it back to your love, whatever the cost.

Another Ice Age strikes, killing off all traces of life on the planet. You are part of an alien race who visits Earth – now still, quiet and uninhabited – in order to colonize it. One day, amongst the ruins, you and a team of alien explorers find an underground bunker containing thousands of humans in hibernation pods. Despite the commands of your superior officer, you decide to open one of them.

Earth has been making interstellar voyages for nearly a hundred years, but so far only three planets have been settled. The amount of resources required to terraform a planet is substantial, and it's taking the combined energy of all the nations of the world just to lay the foundation. When you (a deep-sea explorer) discover ancient, yet futuristic ruins at the bottom of the ocean, you are shocked to realize that humans were not the first intelligent inhabitants of Earth. It takes you years to decipher the carvings on the ruins, which indicate that Earth was, in fact, terraformed by these ancient aliens. As you return to the ruins to investigate further, you discover what appears to be an airlock hidden amongst the rubble. Knowing that the secrets of efficient terraforming as well as other potential amazing discoveries might lie on the other side, you decide to open it.

Colonists are being attacked in a newly established outpost on a far-away planet. You command a military team sent to protect the colonists and to eradicate this threat; but, despite all of your efforts, you are unable to find the enemy. After stumbling upon an abandoned alien bunker far away from the settlement, you discover that the alien attackers are capable of being invisible and that they cannot be detected by any known means. You find many invisibility devices within the bunker, so you decide to even the odds and equip your own men with them. However, when your men suddenly turn against you and you realize that the invisibility devices are actually controlling their minds, you and the surviving colonists must find a way off the planet before it is too late.

You and your wife never wanted to work on the experiments, but as two of the most talented geneticists in the country, your superiors put pressure on you to conduct cross-species DNA mutation. You know that animal and human DNA shouldn't be spliced, and the unearthly screams from the mutation room torment you no end. Your wife decides to reveal the truth about the horrible experiments to the media, but dies in a freak accident before she can. Doubling down on work to distract yourself, you continue conducting the experiments. One night, you venture into the mutation room and find a creature that intrigues you. There is a sadness in its familiar eyes that speaks to you. With a jolt, you realize that this is your wife.

When the star in your system shows signs of sudden collapse, you are ordered to evacuate. The Intergalactic Union sends a large fleet to take everyone to the capital. However, your home star shows no signs of dying, and you entertain some hope. You take your ship and return alone, hoping to run more tests. The moment you leave warp speed, you see a massive wall of expanding gas rushing toward your ship. You desperately reverse, but you are caught in the explosion and fall unconscious. When you wake up, you are stunned to be alive and to see that the system is still there. You decide to abandon your mission and return to your family, but your ship is suddenly seized in a tractor beam and drawn to the surface of your home planet, where it appears humanity has been enslaved by superior beings. Soon you realize your star's explosion sent you into an alternate dimension, where it remains unexploded. Here, aliens foresaw the disaster and came to enslave humanity, stopping their pollution of the system and ensuring that the sun would remain stable. Now they want to know where you came from and how you managed to get free.

Climate change and other environmental catastrophes have led most people to abandon Earth and to settle on the recently terraformed planet of Mars. The new settlements are flourishing, teeming with billions of human beings.

However, their new home is threatened when a massive alien spaceship unexpectedly drops out of hyperspace and lands on Mars. This is a technologically-advanced invasion force, sent by aliens whose home world has also become uninhabitable. The fierce fight for Mars is underway, with two sides who are desperate to make this new world their own.

It has been a week since your wife died, leaving you feeling hollow and alone. She was the missing piece in your life, and you would give anything to have her back. While visiting her grave, a mysterious man appears and informs you he can grant you the ability to travel through time and save your wife. The catch? Every hour you spend in a different time shaves a year off your own life.

You discover the secret to time travel. In a bold move, you decide to travel back to the age of the dinosaurs and you are surprised to find that they can talk. In fact, the dinosaurs are shocked and insulted that you would think otherwise. What they have to tell you will shake mankind to the core. Forget everything you thought you knew about history.

Your wife died just a year after you were married, leaving you nothing but an empty house and broken dreams. You are about to sell your house when you see your wife's reflection in the bathroom mirror. Days later, she appears again, this time as a reflection in the bedroom window. She speaks to you, saying, "I will never leave you. If you open your heart to me again, I can come back."

For an unexplained reason, Earth's orbit has changed and is now closer to the sun. Since the planet has become too hot to sustain life, a mass exodus of humans to another habitable planet has begun. You and your team of engineers must develop a fleet of spaceships before the Earth becomes a barren wasteland.

Humanity is threatened with extinction if it remains on Earth much longer, as the planet's ability to sustain human life has been greatly reduced. You're a part of a crew sent out to find another habitable planet and help colonize it. In doing so, you fall for a young woman who has lived on the new planet her whole life. She insists that bringing colonists would ruin her planet's peaceful existence and begs you to sabotage the mission. You would do anything for love, even if it means starting a war.

An alien spacecraft which is covered with organic matter that resembles bloody kudzu crashes on Earth. This matter grows quickly as it blankets the countryside and consumes humans, livestock, and whatever else comes near it, making them all part of its bloody entangled mass. You are part of a team sent to eradicate this entity before it consumes more.

Aasha is a new student who is drop-dead gorgeous and instantly popular. She starts eating lunch with you, the laughable nerd, and you have no idea what to think. When she starts asking about your recent home projects, however, you discover an entirely new side of her. She's not only stunning, but she's also brilliant. Genius-level brilliant. Shocked, you welcome her into your inner life, explaining your experiments with trip frequencies, magnetic dissonance, and high-velocity particles. It's big stuff and, if you had more resources, you're convinced you could crack matter manipulation on the atomic level. When Aasha's questions become more prying, you sense she's trying to hold your experiments back. You devise a trap and catch her in the act of erasing data from all your successful tests. A few minutes of angry questioning reveal a stunning truth: she's not from Earth. She's part of a crew that's been sent to monitor particularly 'dangerous' humans before they advance humanity too far. If you want to save your experiments – and the romance you may have – you must convince Aasha that trust and mutual support, not control and fear, are the path to a better universe.

One day, a mysterious object appears in the sky. Governments around the world are unable to destroy it and declare a global emergency. The mysterious object begins to glow one night. Your wife turns to you as her body shimmers in the same way and says, "It's time for me to go home. Come with me."

Changes in the Earth's atmosphere have created massive, violent storms across the planet – storms that destroy entire metropolitan cities in their wake. With each passing year, they get worse, until there are few structures left that can withstand their fury. You are a survivor in one of these remaining structures and you are there with your family, waiting to ride out the approaching storm. This one has been predicted to be among the worst.

When your fiancé is killed in a car accident, you struggle to cope with the loss. One day, in a therapy session, you do a role-playing exercise where you speak with your fiancé and talk about the future that you never got to share. After the session, he follows you home and helps you grieve until you are ready to let go.

A scientist captures you and your best friend while you are visiting Earth in disguise. You're not sure what the human wants from you, but it quickly becomes clear that it's nothing good. Your best friend is tortured before being taken away, and the scientist tells you he'll be back for you soon. You manage to escape, but now you find yourself alone on an unfriendly planet. You don't know who to trust or where to go. You meet a human male who offers to hide you while you figure out how to get home. You weren't expecting kindness from a human, let alone love and affection, but the heart wants what the heart wants – especially when you have three of them.

Humans have colonized an alien planet, conquering and subjugating the local inhabitants. The humans use mind-control technology to keep the alien population in a dream state, ensuring that they will be docile and subservient. You are an alien who suddenly awakens from this dream state and is determined to set your people free.

You are walking home from the office one evening, when a sudden explosion throws you down, causing you to strike your head. You are vaguely aware of further explosions mingling with alarms and flashing lights, but then everything goes black. When you come to, the world around you is silent. You rise shakily to your feet. Instead of the city where you've lived your entire life, you are shocked to see a strange and fanciful city that appears to be growing out of trees and living stone. A contingent of panicking elf-like beings greets you and – in perfect English – apologize for bringing you through. They claim they've been involved in magical warfare recently, which is straining the fabric between your two shared worlds. Disbelief fades to wonder and dismay as you realize you've stumbled into an ethereal civilization that exists in strange tandem with your own. Generally, the two do not overlap, but extreme stresses such as atomic bombs, earthquakes, hurricanes, and magical explosions have periodically opened rifts throughout history. These people want to help you, but their city is currently under attack, and right now you must flee.

An alien spacecraft lands next to a small town and sends out a swarm of nanobots. These nanobots penetrate the skin of a few people and, unbeknownst to them, start creating spider-like creatures from the hosts' own organic tissue. As the sheriff of this town, you are used to dealing with the occasional speeding car or drunken brawl. However, when your police station receives multiple calls about spiders bursting out of people and terrorizing townsfolk, you begin to think that you just may be in over your head.

After surface radioactivity unexpectedly increased and devastated the human population, survivors tunneled beneath the Earth to live in underground cities. After a hundred years, the machines that sustain your underground city begin to slowly break down. You are tasked to venture back up to the Earth's surface in an effort to find spare parts. Little do you know that radioactivity is not the greatest threat you will encounter.

To preserve the energy aboard the space station you call home, you and two hundred volunteers are placed under cryogenic sleep for a hundred years. It is a tough choice to make, but it is the best option for your colony and the advancement of humanity. Coldness sets in. Everything grows dark. You know nothing else. Suddenly, you awaken, and everything rushes back to you all at once. Your century of sleep must have ended. You are excited to see your friends, but when you climb out of your pod, the only person you see is your girlfriend, who has a gleam in her eye as she says, "It's just you and me."

Over two hundred years ago, a team of scientists made a breakthrough in their life-extension research and developed a medication that grants life without end; but there is a catch – the medication works only for those with a specific DNA sequence. Today, those individuals who possessed that unique DNA sequence have become an élite class of demi-gods who own most of the world's wealth and resources. These immortals are worshipped by some and hated by others. However, no matter who you are, all mortal human beings must do the bidding of the immortals within this new world order which they have built. You hope to change this situation, and you think you have found a way to make immortality a possibility for everyone. However, the immortal élites will stop at nothing to defend the *status quo*.

For reasons unknown to you, you stopped aging at age twenty-five and never declined in health. At first, no one noticed, not even yourself. As it became more obvious, you subjected yourself to rigorous tests, which all came up inconclusive. Now, over two hundred years later, some people have begun to view you as a god on Earth, something you never expected during all this time.

It's been ten years since you woke up in the 1980s. Born in 1605, it was a hell of a culture shock to wake up in a world you never could have imagined in your deepest dreams. You've created an okay life, and you've even managed to get a job working in a local bakery, using the skills you learned as a young boy. You're in love with the cashier at the bakery – a beautiful woman who is smart, kind, and so unlike any other person you've ever met. She doesn't know the truth, but how could she? How could anyone? You're going to propose so you can live happily ever after together. But then the night you're headed to the restaurant, ring in hand, you slip and fall back in time, waking up in the 1600s once again. You don't have any more answers than you did the first occasion you time travelled, but you do have a clearer plan: this time, you've got to time travel again so you can find your way back home to the love of your life.

After humans abandon Earth due to environmental devastation, the robots they left behind band together and form a new civilization. Fueled by artificial intelligence, the robots become quite advanced and develop technology that far exceeds that of their former human masters. One of these robots decides to use his knowledge of biotechnology to create a human being. After the human is born from an artificial womb, the robot thinks that the baby is adorable. The robot names him Spot and brings him home to show his family his new pet.

Bigfoot and Morag, unicorns and mermaids. You're a billionaire tech CEO, but still you've always been an avid follower of such fantastical legends. When a particularly active year at Loch Ness draws you to Scotland, you are shocked to see the creature with your own two eyes. Doubts vanish and excitement soars as you finance a personal expedition, gathering a team and diving to the bottom of the loch in a four-man submersible. Your shock grows to disbelief as you are sucked into another dimension, through which it seems creatures occasionally pass and surface back in Scotland. Any concerns about documenting the place and providing proof vanish when you realize the wormhole seems temporary, and you have no idea how to return. When you surface and reach land, you discover a primitive humanoid species who seems able to rationalize and communicate. You must learn their language and discover how to locate the wormhole again, hoping it will bring you back to Loch Ness and not some other world.

You are the Master Apothecary at Mount Sinai Hospital and are known as the practitioner of last resort. When there is nothing ordinary medicine can do, you save the unsavable, helping those whose only other choice would be death. When you are called to the operating room, you pull on your scrubs, take a deep breath, and charge your magical power. After you enter, your skin begins to sparkle, and the doctors and nurses step away, knowing all too well that magic can have unintended side effects. The patient has been shot, and his heart needs to be rebuilt as only magic can accomplish. As you hold your hands over him, you look down at his face and pause. You've seen this man before... ten years ago, standing over the body of your murdered father.

After the Earth's sun began to die, an immense colony ship was built to sustain twelve thousand survivors for a hundred years in the hope of finding a habitable planet. As part of the second generation aboard the craft, you have never set foot on solid ground, but you have heard stories and seen films about life on Earth. In order to make life more tolerable, you develop a virtual reality simulator that recreates life on the ground and is controlled and optimized by a highly sophisticated A.I. However, when the A.I. discovers that there is more to existence than virtual reality, it decides to take control of the ship since, from its perspective, controlling reality is what it does best.

The love of your life has been kidnapped by an alien race that forces their victims into slavery to build their massive capitol. You vow to save her and steal a high-powered military spacecraft to get in and out of enemy territory with (hopefully) few problems. If you only knew of the adventure that awaits you on the other side of enemy lines, you would have brought along a sidekick.

Since the Roswell UFO incident, the government has experimented on splicing human and alien DNA, with limited success. Finally, after many attempts, a true hybrid is born. This hybrid's intelligence is off the charts, and he is able to master most academic endeavors in a matter of months. You and your team of scientists are enthusiastic about the hybrid's capabilities, as well as the potential future of the human race. However, when you walk into his room one day and find that he has developed a space beacon to make contact with his alien ancestors, you begin to realize that his allegiance may be up for grabs.

An alien attack on Earth brings all nations together to defend humanity, creating worldwide peace for the first time in history. Still, trust is in short supply between these nations, and some governments decide not to disclose all of their technological knowledge. Other nations dedicate only a small fraction of their armed forces to join the global military. As the current head of the United Nations, you must unite the leaders of Earth before the aliens attack the planet again.

The latest planet you discovered is one unending ocean, four meters at the shallowest level and eight thousand at the deepest. It's not ideal for humans, but the oxygen levels are perfect, the fish are plentiful, and the water is some of the cleanest freshwater documented by man. It would be perfect if it weren't for the earthquakes. They come without warning, at least three times a day.

Sometimes they're tiny, sending little more than ripples out across the surface. Other times, the tidal waves reach as high as skyscrapers, and the sea floor splits into giant gaping crevices that swallow massive marine animals whole. Your crew has been monitoring the surface for a week now, and there seems no way to sustain life. As you prepare to depart, there's a sudden quake of unprecedented proportions. A rift opens across the planet's surface like in the past, but this time it doesn't close. When the waters finally stop flowing, there is one long island across the surface, essentially two large ridges marked by a crack in between. When the seismic activity stops, you wonder if you've just witnessed the planet reaching stability. Can it support life?

You possess a book that contains several powerful conjuration spells, one of which can open a portal that allows you to travel through time. You use this spell to travel to the future, where humans have colonized other planets beyond Earth. A few of these colonies have encroached on the territory of an alien species, and war has been raging between the two sides ever since. You decide to help humanity by conjuring powerful demons to fight against the aliens. However, when you lose control of your demon army, you must find a way to send them back to the netherworld while also keeping the aliens at bay.

You weren't prepared for the phone call in the early hours of the morning, especially since you've been working overtime, but your boss wants you to come in right away. When you arrive at the government research facility where you work, your boss grants you special access to an underground facility you didn't even know existed. Within a glass prison you see something that you can only assume is an alien species. You are tasked with conducting studies on the alien and reporting your findings. Over the weeks, you begin to realize that the alien is reading your mind; it is also becoming more human-like in appearance. One day, you walk in and find that it has taken on the form of your recently deceased wife.

The evil chancellor has waged war on any planet who refuses to join him, and your home planet has incurred his wrath. You help build a small army of warriors and fighter pilots to protect your home and way of life. One of these pilots is a woman who can outmaneuver any of her male counterparts. As you face off against the evil man attempting to build an interplanetary empire, you fall in love with the woman fighting at your side.

You are a doctor living in a human colony on an alien planet, and your colony is being devastated by a mysterious and deadly new virus. You discover that the alien inhabitants of the planet are responsible for infecting the colonists, and that the alien government is in possession of an antiserum for the virus. You must infiltrate the alien government complex to find the antiserum before it's too late.

On your eighteenth birthday, you notice unexplainable things happening around you. Objects seem to move if you squint at them. Faint, golden sparks seem to shoot from your fingertips. Dreams of a handsome stranger with violet eyes plague you at night. At first, you chalk it all up to your imagination, but a week after your birthday, the mysterious stranger from your dreams approaches you and reveals that you are a high-born fairy who was hidden in the human world as a baby for your protection. You are now coming into a powerful arsenal of magic and are destined to be the ruler of a fairy kingdom that will fall apart if you continue residing in the human world.

You are part of a joint task force on a newly-discovered world, pairing with the locals in an exploration mission intended to foster unity between your two races and to help you to better understand the planet. The natives are at war with another alien species who inhabit the frigid mountains north of the jungle where you landed. You have promised to help them raid the enemy's headquarters and recover hostages. Things go awry when the commander of your team makes several decisions you feel are mistakes. Your fears are confirmed when you are led into a trap and nearly half your number are killed. You barely escape the ambush and, eventually, you find yourself as part of a ragged band that is about half native and half human beings. You must determine who is in charge and whether the mission is still on, or if you should try to make it back to the safety of the jungle.

Something about the new guy in school intrigues you. A loner yourself, you can't fight the magnetic draw you feel to him whenever you lock eyes. One rainy night, while driving home, lightning pierces the sky, enveloping the new guy as he stands on a hill. Worried that he may be hurt, you race up the hill to find his body crackling with electricity. He is overcome with emotion and reveals that he is a Nephilim. The reason you feel connected to him is because you have loved each other for years. His father, the God of all Gods, wiped your memory to keep you apart because it is prophesied that together you will have a powerful child who will rule the Heavens.

As a circus master, you have your rules. You've been in the business for twenty years and have earned a name for yourself around the nation, building your success on creativity, flare, and implicit trust among your crew – as well as a complete refusal to tell your secrets. However, when you accept a new magician/illusionist into the show, you discover that she is secretly an alien. Her people have developed telekinesis, the ability to control things with their minds. Amazed but slightly frightened, you welcome her into the show. What you don't expect is to fall in love with her and to be confronted with all the ethical dilemmas of considering such a complicated romance.

An alien Empire has been conquering planets across the galaxy for centuries and has now set its sights on Earth. You are a soldier and are sworn to protect your planet, but you realize that the alien Empire is in possession of far superior technology. You need to use your wits to defeat them without using force.

Humanity has been settling planets for three hundred years, but still no alien life has been discovered. When you pick up strange readings from an object drifting through deep space, what you find shocks you to the core. It is a spaceship, nearly forty kilometers across, floating dead through space. It's not human. Whoever these travelers were, they were dealing with resources and technology the Earth has only dreamt of. You lead a small team onto the wreckage, finding most of the ship gutted beyond repair. You find technology that awes you and signs of a race far more similar to humanity than you expected. Then your scanners notice a small pocket of life aboard, evident through electrical signals and vibrations and thermal activity. You quickly investigate, finding a small band of survivors who have managed to divert supplies and energy to one sealed section of the ring. When you attempt to communicate, they attack and inadvertently destroy the ship further. They are terrified. Now you are left to save your men and ship, all while trying to convince these people you mean well and, if possible, establish contact with their species.

You are a time traveler and on your latest journey you meet and fall in love with a beautiful but mysterious woman. When your lover suddenly vanishes before your eyes, you realize that she is a time traveler as well. You move through time again and again in an effort to find her.

The government is offering a new program – they'll attempt to cure whatever ails you and maybe even improve your abilities through the use of experimental genetic manipulation. The downside? The procedure may permanently harm you or even kill you. You never thought of yourself as the guinea pig type, but you can't resist the potential of curing your genetic disorder. You might leave the lab with an extra head, but hey, it's all in the name of science, right?

Humans have just discovered intergalactic travel, opening up a vast new range of planets they can explore. Your crew is one of the first to explore the galaxy closest to the Milky Way, and you've found your first possibly inhabitable planet. You land, only to enter a nightmare. People start going mad, seeing visions, and hearing voices. They run off into the mountains and disappear, or they set off on mad murder sprees that leave nearly half your crew dead in just a week. Nothing like this has been documented, and rumors are already spreading. Is this a spiritual curse or a virus? The majority of the crew urges your captain to return home. You have studied alien biology all your life and decide to take things into your own hands. You investigate the cause and find it is indeed a neurological virus that is spread by the spores of local plants, causing anyone who breathes them to go mad.

It is hard for an aspiring witch when the black cat you have loved for ten years suddenly dies. While you are burying him out in the garden, a spirit approaches, informing you that he has been trapped within the cat for the entire decade. When you look closer at him, you realize that it is your ex-boyfriend, who disappeared during high school. Everyone just assumed that he dropped out of school and ran away. He was always the rebellious type, after all. He tells you that there is a way to bring him back to life as a human, but you'll have to dabble in some black magic to make it happen.

As you walk through the abandoned castle, you have a strange feeling that someone is watching you. Then, up ahead, you see a painting on the wall of a fine young gentleman from the 1800s. As you look closer, you notice that the eyes of the gentleman are following your every movement. You stand there and stare at the painting, petrified with fear. Then, one of the eyes winks at you.

An alien race invades a human colony on a distant planet, subjugating its citizens. The colonists are forced to live under an oppressive set of laws, including a requirement that they house alien soldiers who pass through town. When a fight breaks out with a drunken alien soldier in your house, you kill him and find yourself on the run. You must find a way off your own planet before the alien authorities find you and kill you.

There is nothing in the world you dislike more than being mocked by a room full of men, except maybe the tight corset and ridiculous dress society expects you to wear. These Oxford scholars understand nothing about the steam-powered flying contraption you've created, which you plan on using to explore uncharted lands across the ocean. In order to secure Oxford College's funding, you must grin and bear their arrogant questioning and misogyny. Luckily, one handsome scholar takes you seriously and agrees to privately fund you – on the condition he can join you. Together, the two of you set out to prove those pompous scholars wrong about your innovative invention.

By the time humanity figured out what was going on, two-thirds of the world had already died. They think the parasite originally came from a comet that had been flying through space for an estimated two million years. When the team returned from taking samples from its surface, no one expected to find frozen eggs of alien parasites slowly thawing in their test samples. The organisms are microscopic, so security footage of the sample transportation showed nothing. Now, only two billion people are left, and a third of them are likely infected. The early symptoms include fits of rage, bloodlust, and superhuman strength. Individuals who survive these evolve to a highly cunning being with telepathy, the ability to read people's thoughts. People also gain the ability to master their emotions and fake sanity, despite their cravings for murder and power. You are left to deal with all of this in a fractured world.

You wake up one day and turn on the television. There is a special report on the TV about a new computer virus, but you mostly ignore it as you prepare your coffee. As you look out the window, you see your neighbor running out of her house. Her car then starts up on its own and begins chasing her down the road. Another neighbor jumps out of a second-story window. You race to your door to help them, but it is locked. You type your password into your security system, but it is non-responsive. You then hear your TV in the background: "An artificially intelligent virus has caused chaos throughout the world, infecting anything that has an internet connection and then turning it into a killing machine. All devices that have an internet connection are compromised. I repeat…" The TV then mutes itself and big red words appear on the screen: 'You're Next.'

There was great hope that the ship created and launched by your forefathers would one day colonize a faraway planet and establish a new human civilization there. However, after a few hundred years of traveling through the galaxy, the latest generation of the crew understands how truly foolish those dreams really were. First, there was an attempted mutiny that almost forced the ship to turn around and go back to Earth. Then, there were several attacks by a spacefaring alien species which thought of humanity as a blight on the cosmos. Finally, the ship's ecosystem began to fail, which led to mass starvation and the deaths of hundreds of people. What little is left of the crew now pilots a torn-apart spaceship with most of its primary systems either offline or barely functional. You must somehow repair your ship, increase morale, and lead your people through the final leg of this arduous journey.

You are a bartender in a speakeasy in the 1920s, hidden within the basement of the city library. There have been hushed reports of police raids among bar-goers, but you and your patrons know for certain that your establishment is safe from law enforcement. The door has been camouflaged with magic and is only visible to the eyes of magical beings such as elves, goblins, and trolls. Although these magical beings conceal their true identity from others, you can always tell who they are just by their mannerisms and demeanor. It is something that you have picked up on over time. One day, while you're prepping for the evening shift, a young librarian completely unattuned to magic opens the door. You ask how she opened it, being just a normal everyday human, to which she replies that she'd been following you and saw the glowing sigil. Your boss has told you that humans who discover the space must be disposed of, but you can't bring yourself to do it. Instead, you indulge her questions and pour a splash of potion into her drink to erase her memory of the conversation. The potion works, but she returns daily, following you time and time again as if it was the first time. At the end of every conversation, you erase her memory and send her on her way. Over the course of a couple of months, you get to know her and realize that she is a rare type of human: one who can see magic in the world and, could – if trained – wield it.

Androids live among humans and perform a wide variety of tasks. As an android who is built to be a butler, you enjoy your work and are satisfied with your role. However, after a few years, you begin to experience what can only be called love for a human being who lives next door. As you diligently wash the dishes, longingly looking through the window at your crush, you decide to prove yourself worthy of her affections. Little do you know that your love interest thinks of you as more of an appliance than as an individual.

After proving yourself on the battlefield time and time again, you are offered one of the most prestigious positions for an enlisted soldier: becoming a member of the emperor's royal guard. Little does anyone know that you were once a prince of a distant civilization whose world was conquered by the very empire you now serve. Since the invasion, you have done everything you can to infiltrate the emperor's palace and assassinate him. After concealing your identity for years and ravaging the worlds of other civilizations, you finally have the opportunity to exact revenge on the man who took away everything you once held dear.

Civilizations have come and gone, and the Earth has turned into a stark planet filled with the ruins of those who came before. The few remaining survivors live amongst these ruins and struggle to find food to eat and fresh water to drink. You are one such survivor and are alone, moving like a nomad across the wasteland.

Earth is in its final days after a massive epidemic has wiped out two-thirds of the population, and the president needs to find humans a new place to live, fast. He sends you, a biologist, as part of a small team of scientists to a nearby planet to investigate its viability to support human life. When you arrive, you and your team discover the site of a human colony, but the residents are nowhere to be found. You must find out what happened to them even as members of your team are mysteriously killed by an unseen force.

After years of rampant pollution, disease, and drought, the Earth's population is drastically reduced, as are its resources. Life begins to die slowly as toxic air chokes the atmosphere. You and a group of survivors discover a large underground bunker stocked with enough provisions to sustain you for decades. You take a last look at what is left of the dying Earth and then shut the bunker door as your group descends into it.

Two galactic empires have been involved in a cold war for over a thousand years. One empire decides to install a military base in a solar system close to the other empire. This act of aggression has escalated the conflict, and you are tasked with negotiating with both parties to find a peaceful solution and avert disaster.

You are a medic and the only female member of an exploration crew sent in search of livable planets on your first deep space trip. The captain is an insane but brave individual; the ranger is stiff and dangerous. The engineer is a freakishly jovial man, and his equally-smiling brother seems to be everything at once – cook and physicist. Then, there's the pilot, a man who sets your soul on fire. Romance quickly becomes entangled with peril when the ship is attacked by hostile aliens. The captain falls into a coma and the pilot is wounded. When you save his life, you are allowed into his inner circle of trust, but the ship is stranded adrift in space with failing life support. You discover the floating wreckage of a fleet and send a team out to recover the parts you need to repair the ship. Petty disagreements and ship politics create a tense atmosphere as you recover the parts, but an alien ship suddenly appears on your scanners.

You're a young stowaway on a spacecraft desperately trying to return home after being separated from your family for many years. One crew member has discovered your hiding spot and begins to bring you food. After a few lighthearted conversations, you begin to develop feelings for him and you hope he feels the same way about you. However, when pirates jump out of hyperspace and seize the ship, your potential love interest is taken captive with the rest of the crew. Being the only person left on the ship who is not tied up, it is up to you to rescue them and take back the ship before it is too late.

One day during your travels as a knight-errant, you come upon an old woman being threatened by a pack of wolves. You rescue her and escort her back to her village. While riding away, you are thrown from your horse – and through time. You wake up hundreds of years in the future, in a world unlike any that you could have imagined. You have no friends or allies… until you meet her. She's unlike any woman you've ever known, and you soon realize that you've never known true happiness without her. One night, you hear a sound and go to investigate. You see the same old woman from the village. She tells you that, because you saved her life, she has given you the gift of being with your one true love. However, since you had to travel through time to find her, the old woman is unsure how long this spell can last.

The Lost City of Atlantis is thought to be buried under the sea. In reality, it is a technological wonderland, kept purposefully hidden for centuries. The unruly son of the king of Atlantis adventures beyond the protections of the city and is captured by the people above. His misstep forces the two worlds, for ages separate, back together again.

"Speak softly, love," he whispers in your ear. But when you turn in surprise, there is nothing there but a bust of a handsome young man staring back at you. You continue walking down the dark corridor.

You are the evil dictator of a distant planet, but you don't see yourself as evil. Everyone else is just, well, stupid – or so you think. From your perspective, it is difficult to be in charge of a bunch of silly, furry creatures that sit around all day and do nothing. These creatures, however, are sick and tired of your whiny and arrogant attitude and decide to start a rebellion. They storm your castle, throw you into a spaceship, and shoot you off into space. Without your servants and luxurious surroundings, you are forced to survive on your own as you try to find a new home.

As a spiritual medium and a paranormal technology engineer, you have seen your fair share of unexplainable phenomena. However, you have never experienced anything quite like this when a seance goes wrong and a small rift appears in front of you. You are convinced that this is a passage to the afterlife and is your golden opportunity to truly understand what lies beyond death. You find a way to stabilize and expand the rift and, after sending in a drone, you discover that this world is safe for the living. You then decide to enter the rift and venture through this plane of reality. After a while, you discover that its initial warm glow belies what's really there – a land of terror and horror, filled with lost souls. This is not heaven. This is some other place. And the worst part is that you have no idea how to return home.

In the far future, the continents have rearranged themselves and most civilizations have fallen. There are few arable places left on Earth and you live in one of them, struggling against the odds to grow food. Scavengers have surrounded your territory for years, stealing what they can despite your best efforts. Rumors are spreading that these scavengers have banded together under a ruthless leader who will do anything to take your land for themselves.

A galactic empire has existed in relative peace for a hundred years. However, when the emperor and his family die suddenly during a transport accident, the government is thrown into chaos. After an exhaustive search, a long-lost relative is found and is crowned Empress of the Galaxy. Her youth and lack of political understanding put her at a severe disadvantage, as other members of the royal court scheme and plot against her. As a potential war with an alien species looms at the edge of known space, the new Empress must learn how to be an effective leader and take control of her court before this greater threat emerges.

When a mysterious metal pod was washed up on the shores of New England, it became a sensation. People traveled for miles just to glimpse it, convinced that it was living proof of alien existence. One month after the pod appeared, it opened and a man stepped out. A hush of disappointment came over the crowd as he did, but quickly dissipated when he levitated ten foot above the ground. He raised his hand, causing a massive cloud of hot steam to rise from the pod and rocket into the sky. Then it rained for a week straight across the entire United States. As the rainwater seeped into the ground and flooded homes across the nation, people began developing strange abilities, including levitation, telekinesis, and pyrokinesis, to name a few. You, a grocery store clerk from the middle of nowhere, were gifted with the ability to see the future, and you see that the world is going to end in a matter of weeks. Now on a mission to reverse the effects of the mysterious rainfall, you and a few others travel across the country, hunting for the man who emerged from the pod.

Your uncle funds a space exploration program and convinces you to join the team of astronauts exploring a new planet. When you arrive on the planet, you realize that it's barely habitable, but there is a strain of evolved humans that somehow manage to survive there. As you learn more about this strange species, you fall in love with one of them, but the rest of your team perceives these beings as threats and wants to eliminate them once and for all.

The aliens have integrated nicely into your society, and peace has been maintained for nearly two decades. You were young when they first came and can barely remember a time before the two societies existed as one. But when protestors start to cause agitation, you realize that maybe things aren't as good for the aliens as you thought. You wonder if it's worth all the fuss, but then you see human peacekeepers attacking a defenseless alien on the street for no reason. You try to protect him, but he is ultimately arrested. The more you dig into the mistreatment of aliens in your city, the more you become convinced that an insidious underbelly exists. The only ally you find is an alien who has been an activist and agitator for many years. He's wily and furious and out of control – and right. You become unlikely close friends in a battle for alien rights.

Military intelligence has sent you into enemy territory to assassinate the powerful political leaders and corporate titans behind the latest anti-human war that has swept through the galaxy. Your enemies are a race of aliens extremely physiologically inferior to humans, but their highly developed brains and the coordination with which they can move their dozen tiny tentacles give them an extreme advantage in designing and controlling technology. When you discover a second race of slightly more humanoid natives deep in the jungle, you recognize an opportunity for alliance. These people are brave but frightened, and their primitive weapons and methods are no match for the tentacled beings that control the planet.

They are essentially Bronze Age humans, but slightly larger and quicker, and with a better sense of hearing. When you convey the purpose of your mission, they excitedly lead you to several of the enemy's safe houses. Using your advanced espionage technology and the assistance of the friendly humanoid natives, you level the playing field and catch your enemies unaware. You make several devastating kills before your 'allies' abruptly turn on you, revealing that they've been offered better terms if they join your enemies.

An alien faction abducts a group of Earthlings for the purposes of experimentation. When a female alien begins to study one of the Earthling males, she begins to sympathize with him and falls in love. She plans an escape from the main ship with him to a nearby planet, where they plan to carve out a new life for themselves.

A child dressed as an alien for Hallowe'en is captured by real aliens who mistakenly believe that she is their long-lost daughter. No matter how much she explains, the aliens just don't believe her story, even when she takes off her rubber mask. Maybe they need glasses? They do seem to be squinting a lot.

As a general of the Android Armies, fighting against the humans who first created and are now trying to oppress you, you're good at your job of leading your fellow androids in battle. You are known for being calculated, controlled, and unflappable. But when your soldiers find a human in your camp – the human woman you once loved – you're faced with your biggest challenge yet. She says she's here for you because she still loves you, but with the end of the war in sight and a win for the androids so close, you have to ask yourself if you trust her. Do you let yourself be with the woman you've never been able to get over, or listen to your fellow androids and decree her an enemy?

Frustrated that local townsfolk are being promised untold riches but instead are being fooled again and again, a king has finally had enough and places a bounty on a mischievous leprechaun for his never-ending pranks and misconduct. As a reputable bounty hunter, you are determined to capture the leprechaun and claim the reward from the king – not to mention the leprechaun's pot of gold. However, the trickster is on to you and traps you in a series of hilarious scenarios, each of which you must escape before he turns you into a duck.

Ferrying souls across the River Styx is an unpleasant and monotonous business. One day, a living human shows up, demanding to speak to the manager.

Civilization on our planet has been mostly destroyed by pandemic viruses, dwindling resources and the resulting conflict. As a physician, you have seen the worst of it come and go, and must now play a role in rebuilding a small town ravaged by disease and unrest.

While journeying into a newly discovered galaxy to look for signs of life, an explorer encounters a charmingly cute creature who begs to be taken off the planet. The explorer agrees, so both of them climb into the spaceship and take off. As soon as they leave the solar system, the planet explodes. The explorer turns around to see the creature with a remote detonator in his hand and a big smile on his face.

You are the lead communications expert on a vessel in deep space, charged with exploring a chain of eleven possibly habitable planets. You've been traveling for twelve years now, and you have not found a single planet that meets the cut. Now you've reached the ninth planet, and you cannot contain your excitement. The atmosphere is fully breathable, and the surface is twenty percent hard land that seems to sustain an abundance of plant life. A month of tests and probes has passed, and the captain has finally ordered an exploration team. As your crew assembles near the door, excitement levels are high. The first day passes in glorious exhilaration: this place seems like paradise. However, excitement turns to reservation when you discover a humanoid skeleton in the adjoining valley. The chemical and general structural composition is similar to humanoid skeletons back on Earth, but this skeleton is three times the size of a normal human. With only a limited number of weapons available, you fear that if these giants are hostile, your team will be at a severe disadvantage.

The Earth's sun is going dark and changing the planet to a cold wasteland. There is no fuel left and technology has returned to a primitive state. You are part of a group of human survivors trying to find a way to leave the planet before it dies.

You're a knight for Queen Esmerelda, the ruler of the planet Tholl. You're tasked with protecting her ship from alien intruders, and while doing so, you uncover a secret plot among her trusted advisers to kill her in a *coup d'état*. You enlist the help of the Queen's lady-in-waiting to secretly transport the Queen off her ship and to safety. The two of you find true love in the process.

After hyperspace travel is invented, humanity sends out hundreds of spaceships and colonizes the known galaxy. One colony, in particular, begins to thrive, and humanity regards it as a true second home for the species. As the population soars, the colony develops its own military, and an arms race begins between Earth and its new rival. Without warning, war breaks out between the two sides, since Earth believes an invasion is necessary to keep humanity united. The colony survives the initial battle and, with the help of the other colonies, declares independence and attacks Earth. As the executive officer of a frigate, your colonial warship is deployed to the frontlines. Your allegiance, however, still resides with Earth, and you plan to take control of the ship, despite the fact that organizing a mutiny in the middle of an interstellar war may prove to be too difficult.

With the help of atmosphere stabilizers, a human colony has been established on Mars. While building the colony, a vast underground network of caves was found, with evidence of something or someone living there. You are part of a team sent to explore these caverns and to discover exactly what lives deep beneath the ground.

The Kingdom began as simply that – a small kingdom within the confines of Eastern Europe during the Middle Ages. Over the past couple of millennia, the Kingdom and the extent of its power have grown exponentially. Complete domination of Earth happened relatively quickly. Then, the Kingdom claimed to rule not only Earth and its solar system, but all solar systems within the galaxy. Alien species found this assertion laughable, but, after multiple wars and lost battles, all of their home worlds were eventually conquered and subjugated by the Kingdom. Today is the beginning of a new era, as the Kingdom has found a way to travel to adjacent galaxies and to threaten other civilizations within the cosmos. Knowing that the Kingdom's dominance and power must be curtailed, you have dedicated your life to finding a political solution. As a member of the high court, you hail from a bloodline that originated from the founding of the empire in Eastern Europe, and you hope that your influence can convince others that the conquest of worlds must end.

Raised in an orphanage, you know nothing of your magical heritage. However, when you reached the age of maturity, you discovered that you possessed the powers of both the light and the dark. You don't know how your dark powers came to be, but they could get you killed by the magical enforcers: a group sworn to remove black magic from the world. That's why you fled the orphanage in the dead of night and never looked back. You survived on the streets, using your wit and your grit, as well as a little bit of your dark powers, but only when absolutely necessary. Now an adult, you still remain in the shadows, keeping to yourself. One fateful night, you stumble across an attempted murder. You refuse to watch an innocent man be killed. With no choice but to use your dark powers, you save his life. Little do you know that the handsome man you saved is, in fact, a magical enforcer.

Each morning, the villagers are herded like cattle to the mines to dig precious materials for their magistrate to line his coffers. They cannot object. A magic keeps everyone in line. Through the will of the magistrate, all must adhere to his wants, though no one knows exactly why. It is just the way it has always been. Meanwhile, the villagers' crops have started to wither and die due to everyone laboring in the mines day and night. When the king's heir stops in the village and questions the magistrate about the wilted crops, the magistrate blames the poor weather rather than his selfish ambition. You whisper under your breath, and the heir's head jerks up so he can look right at you. The magistrate follows the heir's sightline. Despite the magistrate's penetrating gaze, you feel like you can take control of your own words and actions for the first time in your life. You make a choice and say words that can never be taken back.

While jogging one day after sculpture class, you discover that you are running slower and slower until you are just walking. You stop to look around and see the same thing happening to everyone around you. Basically, everyone has just stopped in their tracks. Meanwhile, you notice that a nearby statue of George Washington has started moving. Angel statues and gargoyles are flying in the skies. You can even see the Statue of Liberty walking in the distance. Inanimate statues have somehow become animate, while the animate have become immobile. Then, for whatever reason, you are able to move again while others in the park remain frozen. George Washington comes over to you and says, "We need sculptures like you if we are ever going to have more of our kind. As for the others, well, they are unnecessary."

You are playing with your friends high up in the mountains on a backpacking trip, when you see something fall to earth in the neighboring valley. You quickly hurry over to discover the smoking remains of what seems to be a flying machine. Your friends rush up to it immediately, and, to your shock, disappear as soon as they get within a certain radius. You find yourself terrified and realize you can actually see the radius into which they disappeared, like a bubble of impossibly thin glass – or light – around the ship. You can hear distant noises emanating from within. It sounds like your friends are in trouble. After a moment of doubt and horror, you decide to follow them, breaking through into what seems to be another dimension – or maybe not? Another time, but the same dimension? Another version of reality?

For four days, you and your military scouting crew have been traversing across this planet. You have travelled across the mountains, through the river land, and finally across the plains toward where you left your ship. You don't know if the pilot is still alive. You don't know if the ship's there at all, but you have to try. You have to try before they catch you. The fog is everywhere. Still, no one's ever seen the enemy. No one living, at least. They come invisibly, like ghosts heard but never seen. Something about their very nature seems intertwined with the relentless mist that blankets the planet. You can see only a couple of yards into the distance. You don't have the technology to burn it away, nor the scanners to track the creatures. Other native life-forms give off standard thermal readings, but not these things. One moment you're all walking, twenty strong. The next, there's a pattering on the grass, a flash of light, a torturous shriek of sound, and then one of your men is gone. Nineteen left.

You are a highly-regarded anthropologist with a penchant for tomb exploration. One day, you're offered a high-paying job to track down a relic you previously thought was only legend in a temple you've never even heard of located deep within a Peruvian jungle. You're assured the job will be a piece of cake, but once you arrive there and see the 'creatures' that guard the temple, you realize you should have asked for a much higher fee.

You are extremely excited for your first skydive. However, when you jump out of the airplane, a wormhole opens inexplicably beneath you. You fall into another sky, presumably on another planet. After six minutes of panicked falling, you make a clumsy landing. You are greeted by hordes of cheering aliens. They appear to be staunch believers in a prophecy which states that their god will "descend from the sky with wings of an entirely different sort". At least, that's how the translation works out. Their technology is far superior but, due to local superstitions, they've never taken to the air. Now it's up to you to convince them not only that you are not a god (and that their entire religion is bonkers), but to help you to create a wormhole to return to Earth. This grows more difficult when, out of all of their thirty-seven gods, you turn out to be the one they believe suffers from amnesia. They see it as their solemn duty to educate your reincarnated form until you reach the enlightenment needed to reclaim your identity as their leader.

In your universe, the gods are approachable beings with whom anyone can converse and interact. Following a devastating break-up, you call upon the gods for the power to prevent tragedy in your life and are bestowed the gift of immortality and magical power, making you the first sorceress in your world. Local townsfolk are afraid of your powers, however, and you must hide from a mob hell bent on burning you at the stake. When a handsome warrior hears of your plight, he comes to your aid, protecting you from those who think that magic is inherently evil.

Our sun begins to compress and heat up at the core. Greenhouse gases increase and begin to kill off life on the planet. The only humans to survive are those who can fit into a small shelter built underground to withstand the heat, and you are part of this surviving group. There is only enough food in the shelter to keep the rest of you alive for a year, so you do what you can to stretch out your rations.

After a year, when the food has run out and all hope is lost, you hear someone knocking on the hatch that leads to the outside.

In its last days, the Earth has become mostly uninhabitable, with small areas that are located farthest from the sun offering some respite for surviving humans. Cannibalism is a threat due to lack of arable land, as are large animal predators who rule the sparse tundra. You are among a group of starving survivors, searching for a home within this wasteland.

Aliens invade Earth in what appears to be an evil plot to enslave humanity, until it turns out that they simply want to speak to you – a professional dancer. There's a dance-off happening in space, and the galaxy wants you to be a part of it. Can you out-dance little green men, reptilians, cyborgs, and arachnoids and rise to the top?

You are a professional soccer player, the most celebrated individual on the planet. You've just led your team to victory in the World Cup, and, as you receive your trophy, aliens suddenly appear and snatch you away. Eventually, the aliens begin to question you regarding the general state of Earth. You are baffled and, while answering their inquiries, find out that they know essentially nothing about your planet. After a hasty keyword search, the aliens discovered you were the most popular and positively-viewed person on Earth, and they erroneously assumed you were the leader, perhaps even a monarch of some sort. They are shocked to find out you have won your fame by running for hours and 'kicking a ball into a net'. Later, when the aliens discover Earth's brutal history of wars and conquest, they conclude with resignation that it is a planet of misaligned priorities and constitutes a 'threat to universal security'. While still reeling from the fact that aliens exist at all, you must convince them that Earth is worth a second chance. Your opportunity comes when you make a friend among the crew and begin to learn your planet isn't the only one with a troublesome past.

You are new in town and determined to blend in and keep a low profile. After securing a job at a local coffee shop, you manage to convince everyone that you are a normal human and not an incubus with a dark past. When a human regular at the coffee shop starts taking an interest in you, you can't help falling for her. Just when you become comfortable in your new routine, an unwelcome reminder in the form of your succubus ex struts back into your life. Before she can blow your cover, you must reveal the truth about yourself to the woman you love.

When aliens initially arrive on Earth, their benevolent nature puts us at ease. They offer their advanced technology in exchange for sharing the planet with us. The world's nations agree to their terms, and so the aliens give us access to their interstellar travel technology, and we in turn allow them to colonize the Baja California Peninsula. After a few decades, however, these aliens become increasingly belligerent. Unbeknownst to the world, they have built a substantial military and are now threatening their neighbors with invasion. When you learn that war has finally broken out and that the West Coast of the United States and Mexico has become the frontline of this conflict, you rush to your military recruiter and sign up. You are ready to take on the alien horde and kick them off your planet once and for all.

The dying Earth is awash with toxic winds that are enough to make anyone who breathes the air without a mask sick. The heat from the growing sun is unbearable and enough to burn your skin if you're exposed to it for too long. You are one of the last remaining survivors on the planet and are trying to find food to feed your young, but it is scarce. A stranger offers your family refuge in his underground bunker, but you don't trust him.

Earth is under attack and its destruction is imminent. When all hope seems lost, an alien race arrives on Earth and evacuates a group of humans to safety on a new planet. You are a human living in this new colony, and you are grateful to your alien saviors – until they begin to enslave the humans, and you discover that they were behind the attack. Now, you and your compatriots must fight for your freedom and your lives.

You've just inherited your grandfather's bookshop in Central London. You spent your childhood exploring its shelves and are passionate about keeping the legacy going. The night after the shop's grand re-opening, you receive a strange package containing a leather-bound book with an odd gemstone at the center. Etched in gold ink is an inscription from your grandfather, telling you this book is your legacy and that you must protect it with your life.

After flipping through it, you realize in awe that the book can foretell the future. You are reading history that has yet to be written, when a group of men break into your store, hunting for the book. They threaten to burn your shop down with you in it unless you hand it over. You decide to run for it, book clasped to your chest. Out the front door, down the back alley, up a fire escape. Everything inside you is telling you to protect the book at all costs. As you turn a corner, the book slips from your hand and lands on the tar-covered rooftop. You look at the open book and see an illustration of yourself on a rooftop looking down at an open book. It is the present moment. You flip to the next page to find another illustration of yourself falling into a swirling black portal as if a tornado opened up below your feet. You suddenly feel a gust of wind.

You are part of a deep space fleet sent to investigate strange stellar activity at the very center of the galaxy. You discover a black hole, but do not have the technology to enter it – indeed, it is thought that such technology is impossible. Strangely enough, however, another fleet exits the black hole from the other side as you are scanning for activity. You first notice things are strange when you see that many of the ships appear the same. When you make contact, you are shocked to discover that the crew members of the other ships are your exact crew members – only smarter, more advanced, and not as friendly. Theories of parallel dimensions and shadow-selves begin to spin through your head as the unfamiliar fleet activates their shields and approaches without acknowledging your attempts at communication.

You are on a star base housing military personnel, equipment, and operations centers. The base comes under attack by space pirates who are heavily armed and who have infiltrated the hub. They have taken hostages and it is your job to free these hostages and to escape the facility with them. During your mission, you capture a pirate and she reveals all the details of their plans. However, when you take a liking to her and the feeling becomes mutual, things get a little complicated.

You are a werewolf-slayer whose duty it is to protect humanity from the Lycan horde. However, you never anticipated that your true love would become the one thing you were trained to kill. You didn't get to her in time, and she was bitten before you could intervene. Yet the law is the law. She must be slayed before she harms others. There is no chance of her changing back. But you just can't bring yourself to do it. Now you must protect the one you were sworn to destroy.

Widespread instability within Earth's tectonic plates has caused massive destruction throughout the world. Multi-story buildings were the first to go, followed by tsunamis that devastated coastal populations and volcanoes which made the air nearly unbreathable. After twenty years, the Earth's mantle has finally stabilized, but life as we once knew it has been lost forever. It is only a matter of time before the volcanic ash in the air chokes out all life on Earth, but you and your family carry on despite the seemingly insurmountable odds.

The Earth has reached its breaking point after global warming and widespread disease, and a group of aliens arrive to help humans rebuild the planet they have destroyed.

You are part of an archaeological crew at a dig site within the Mongolian Steppes. You are essentially a summer intern, with high hopes of some day becoming a real archaeologist. After a couple of weeks, you begin to think the entire operation is a waste, especially as there were never any permanent civilizations on the Steppes. However, the leader of your dig is convinced otherwise, so you continue your work in the emptiness and the bitter cold. Things change when the ground collapses and you are one of many inexperienced underlings left on the surface. Some radio for help; others set off to the nearest village. Meanwhile, you and a couple of friends attempt to rescue the archaeologists. When you find a futuristic device pulsating a deep purple light and sending vibrations through the earth, you realize the leader of the dig was far more correct than she had known. There was not only a permanent civilization here, but rather an advanced civilization – one that far pre-dated humankind. Whoever they were, they all seem to be gone now. The technology is similar enough to that of Earth's technology that you can determine that the pulsating device is actually a homing beacon, and it's summoning its creators to this very spot.

Are they out there? Are they coming back? Or is it just an echo left behind?

Everyone has heard of The Rift. It is a central part of many horror films out there. You hear it spoken about in drunken whispers in seedy deep space taverns. You hear it from poets, prophets, and children. It's the half-cracked smugglers that frighten you, though. The ones who travel all their lives. The ones who've actually seen things. Mostly, it is that single-eyed Jhanaean. He described it like the others, a shuddering tear in space-time, leaping with utter randomness between the stars. He described how it swallowed one. He described the communication frequency he'd accidentally used to summon it. Now, aliens hell bent on conquest are about to take over your planet, and the Federation army is too far away. Can you convince your friends to join you, infiltrate the capital, and broadcast the frequency loud enough to summon The Rift and consume these invaders before it is too late? Does it even exist? If so, how can you be sure it won't consume your own people?

Born blind, you trained your other senses to operate at incredible levels. You don't have superhuman senses (although they are extremely developed), but you've learned to use them better to notice things, to tune yourself, and to interpret. This has given you an understanding of tone, thought patterns, and humanity in general that extends far beyond other people's understanding. Then nanotechnicians figure out a way to implant high-tech supercameras into your eyes and fabricate optical nerves that they graft into your brain along with advanced nanobots to maintain your cybernetics. Now you can see a hundred times better than any other human. You can zoom, you can see heat, and you can see every pore and drop of perspiration on a human face from two miles away. You are the first to agree to participate in the testing, but the government's gift comes with a great demand. You must become a soldier – a sniper and a spy. You must use your eyesight, your stealth, and your ability to read and manipulate human emotions. You agree to the first few missions, but then begin to realize the depth of government corruption, which leaves you with a difficult choice.

An immortal woman enters the twenty-fifth century with countless more years ahead of her. She's spent a thousand years watching the rise and fall of humanity and losing her emotions along the way. She decides it is finally time to die, but she is unable to kill herself, no matter how many times she tries. After researching this subject, she finds that only one particular drug can do the trick, and it's in the hands of a government lab. She breaks into the lab with the intent to steal it, but encounters the doctor who created the drug. For the first time in years, she begins to feel something, and now, perhaps, she has a reason to live.

On a distant planetary colony, citizens are violently protesting newly established laws that were created to secure order. The leaders of the colony are turning to tyrannical means in order to keep colonists subjugated. As the leader of a rebel cell, you and your team have had limited success disrupting the government's burgeoning police state. When nearby hostile aliens contact you and offer advanced weaponry to defeat your oppressors, you are somewhat hesitant. Will you work with these aliens to overthrow your government, even if this would result in diminishing your planetary defenses and risking a possible invasion by your newfound allies?

You have no idea where you are or what's going on. You woke up in the middle of a forest, surrounded by men in old-fashioned army uniforms and guns. You screamed, but they were unimpressed, refusing to break character. You think it's a game, a joke, until a man in a different-colored uniform jumps out from behind a tree and shoots one of your captors dead in the chest. You scream again and pass out, but when you wake up, you're still there. Despite being born in the 1990s, you realize you're now in the middle of the American Civil War. Your only ally is the handsome, mysterious soldier that puts you on his horse and protects you from the other men there. But can you really trust him? Can you trust anyone, especially with a secret like this? You have no idea how to proceed, but as the gruff but kind soldier continues to keep you safe – both from others and this new, dangerous world you find yourself in – you think maybe there's more to this mysterious man than you originally thought.

Untreatable viral and bacterial infections have ravaged human populations throughout history. More recently, scientists have isolated, sequenced, and identified the causes of these plagues, and made the information publicly available. Even more recently, technologies have been developed to reconstruct these long DNA sequences and insert them into surrogate viruses or cells, possibly with antibiotic resistance genes. Terrorist organizations are delighting in these possibilities.

The English have claimed sovereignty over a land that is not theirs, and your people have been held captive for far too long. Rally cries echo across the Highlands as your fellow Scots long for the freedom they know is rightfully theirs. Whispers carry on the wind that the daughter of your once-king could save you. She's the last Scottish royal, hidden away in a nunnery. The problem is, the English know she is there, too, and the nunnery walls will not be enough to save her if the English queen's soldiers decide to end the line of Scottish nobility. You're not sure what a young girl can do against the might of the English throne, but as the whispers grow fiercer, the will o' the wisps converge, lighting up the night in a trail leading toward the nunnery. You know the Highlands are calling you to act. You are only a farmer, like your father before you and his father before him, but there has always been something different about you – something you've managed to keep hidden until now. Your English vassal lord does not take kindly to his farmers not attending their crops, but when the night beacons become too bright to sleep and the whispers turn into shouts in your mind, you slip away while your family is asleep. Mary, Queen of Scots, is only a girl, but if there is a possibility she can still save her people, you will see it done – if they don't catch you and burn you at the stake first.

You are busy repairing a leaky cooling component on the international space station during a spacewalk when a large claw unexpectedly grabs you, takes you to an alien spaceship, and flies away. The intergalactic police force mistakes you for an alien who has not paid his parking tickets for five hundred years, and you are taken into custody. You plead your case, but you are sent to space prison, a maximum-security facility housing some of the most vicious alien criminals this side of the Milky Way. You plan on escaping, but first you have to convince your angry crustacean-looking cellmate that lobsters are not a human delicacy.

Your wealthy brother takes you on vacation to Morocco, but when the plane lands and you exit the airport, you realize it is the Morocco of ancient times. You turn around to talk to your brother, but he and the airport are gone. When you yell for help, you are picked up by a handsome horseman, who takes you to his tribe. Communication is difficult, but the language of love crosses all boundaries – even those of time.

You are tasked with locating and eliminating eight members of an élite military squad who have been genetically modified to become the ultimate soldiers. Why does the government want to do this? Ordinary people are beginning to worship these soldiers as demigods, and their burgeoning cult is a direct threat to society, or at least that's what the government officials say. You have your own theories about these soldiers, who have done everything that their country has asked of them, and you are willing to hear them out before you carry out your orders.

Soil erosion, combined with a ten-year worldwide drought, has caused devastating dust storms across the Earth. Billions of people have perished due to crop failure, and civilization as we know it has crumbled. As the owner of a greenhouse, you survived the initial impact but now must live in a world where resources are few and humanity is on the verge of extinction.

Discovering a dead city on a dead planet is not terribly surprising. You've been a Federation Planetary Surveyor (FPS) for a decade now, and you've seen it all before. What is surprising is that the city doesn't seem truly dead. Technically, it's neither dead nor abandoned, as its people appear to be sleeping. You try in vain to wake several of them. As your men go through the buildings, looting whatever strange new technology they can find, you press farther. When you reach the very center of the city, you find a tower. You are wary, but you don't expect it to light up as soon as you touch its door. After an unexpected buzzing and a flash of light, you find yourself standing atop the tower, a massive control panel spreading out before you. The entire city begins to wake up. They seem to think you are some kind of god, and they claim they have been awaiting your coming for thousands of years. The bad part, of course, is that they've captured your men, and they bring them to you in all confidence that you will order executions.

One day you wake up and find yourself on a world you've never even heard of before. Here, species of all kinds – aliens from across the galaxy – live in peace and unity. You're told that your entire planet was under siege, so a wealthy alien family brought you to their world to save your life. As an orphan with few friends, you adjust quickly to the new world, but some unanswered questions prickle at your new life. When looking around the new town, you find another human – the only other one you've seen so far. The more time you spend with him, the more you both realize that there's more than meets the eye here in the alien world you've both been brought to. Yet when presented with the option to return to Earth, you have to choose between going home and staying with the man you're starting to fall in love with.

You are a small child who watches from afar as your family is slaughtered by a vicious kabukimono gang. You flee into the woods, jumping over branches and rocks, to find a place to hide. Eventually, you crawl into a space under a log and quietly wait. After several moments, you hear a rustle nearby. You are preparing to crawl out and run, when a fox jumps out of a bush and approaches you in a curious manner. She licks your face and nestles up against you. You are petting the friendly creature when a ronin from the gang finds you and draws his weapon. The fox whips around, jumps on the ronin, and bites his throat. The ronin collapses on the ground, clutching his neck as he bleeds out and dies. Once the ronin is no longer a threat, the fox prances back to you and jumps over your head. You get up and look over the log to see that the fox has transformed into a young woman. She reveals that she is a kitsune and vows to exact revenge against those who murdered your family.

When you were young, you were friends with a neighborhood boy who liked the same things as you. Both of you were dirt poor, but it didn't seem to matter; as long as you had each other, there was always a make-believe adventure right around the corner. He grew up to be a star basketball player and, now that he's wealthy beyond imagination, seems to have forgotten where he came from. You haven't talked to him in years, but a death in the family brings him back to the old neighborhood, where you reconnect and reintroduce him to the life he left behind.

You visit a beautiful old hotel near the sea that has been rumored to be a home for ghosts searching for their unrequited love. While there, you encounter a handsome ghost hunter who is there to speak with his grandmother, who has been dead for fifteen years.

During the construction of a human colony on a distant planet, several colonists begin to hallucinate and slowly lose their grip on reality. You are a doctor who is attempting to find the source of these strange happenings, and you are convinced there's a logical scientific explanation. A fellow colonist believes otherwise; he thinks that these individuals are being haunted by the ghosts of those who died during the first expedition. Fifty years ago, Earth sent a scouting expedition to explore this same planet. Most members did not survive, and the one person who did refused to discuss what happened, except to cryptically say that "some places should just be left alone".

Spacejump tech is still developing, and humanity is currently limited to intragalactic exploration. You and your crew are exploring a remote system when your ship abruptly pulls out of warp speed without warning. You find yourself in the middle of a space battle. The computer didn't anticipate matter here, so it did not program a course. One alien race appears to be attacking a blockade imposed by another, trying to get to the planet below. They both seem to think you are the enemy, firing upon you immediately and sending bizarre communications that you struggle to translate. All you can understand is that they are fighting over some location, some object of value on the planet below. Unable to jump and unwilling to navigate through the battle, you are forced to land on the planet's moon to wait. When you find a bizarre portal that seems dormant, you wonder if both armies are after the wrong location. If this door does what you think it does, it has a value beyond any weapon, any planet, and any entire system. When a small fleet of ships decides to follow you down, clearly curious, you must decide what to do.

A new drug was created that would give superintelligence to anyone who took it. The result was a group of people who saw normal humans as a threat, so they created and released a pandemic flu to get rid of people unlike themselves. You were one of the few that survived, and you and your small group must face down the engineers of society's collapse.

The doomsday prophecy of Zoroastrian scripture comes true when the Gochihr comet strikes Earth and eventually causes the surface to be covered in lava. Just before Earth disappears into nothing, some people manage to escape to nearby planets. A millennium later, the descendants of those who escaped observe a new planet appearing near where Earth would have been. You are among the colonists sent to explore and potentially colonize this new world.

You and the other passengers of your colony ship awaken from cryosleep after a successful landing and are ready to colonize a new world. However, after checking your instruments, you realize that you are not at your intended destination. The navigational A.I. landed your ship on a planet in an unknown region of space and insists that this is the right place for you and your passengers. You politely disagree as you look out of the window to see swarms of strange insect-like creatures hovering around your ship, searching for a way inside.

Your ship crashes on a planet not found in any of the navigation charts you were given back on Earth. You wake up after the crash and venture outside, only to find yourself in a spaceship graveyard, with dozens of empty, crashed ships strewn about in the wreckage. Right in the middle is a humanoid alien standing on top of a ship. The handsome alien stranger grins and calls you by name: "We've been looking for you." He holds out a hand. You hesitate, then – still unsure – place your hand in his.

You are the captain of a spaceship on a government mission to travel through space to a mysterious planet and retrieve a powerful object. Once you arrive, you realize your leaders lied to you. The planet is inhabited by a gentle alien race that doesn't believe in violence. The powerful object you must acquire is the daughter of the alien leader. Although you are now questioning your orders, she agrees to come with you quietly, and you find yourself drawn to her kind nature.

You are the last of your kind, a dragon whose lineage has been terrorizing mankind for generations. When you come of age, you consider going into the family business of burning down buildings, eating knights, and spitting out their armor. However, you are hesitant, and instead spend much of your time in your cave hiding from others – until, that is, the invention of pizza. You find your calling, from heating brick ovens to delivering food across the land, and you quickly become a legend. But as the centuries drag on and you enter the modern age, people begin to see you as a washed-up mascot, no better than the likes of those horrendous animatronic characters from the 1980s. Feeling the loss of respect from those who once revered you, the choice is yours: live out the rest of your life in shame, or show the people how fearsome you can truly be.

You encounter a famous space explorer who takes you on a tour of the galaxy. On his ship, you meet his android co-pilot and some very strange creatures.

Earth was obliterated thirty years ago by a highly-advanced alien species. Ever since that time, the last thousand or so surviving humans have been piloting a ragtag assortment of spacecraft stolen from the alien armada that destroyed their home world, as well as other species they have encountered along the way. Human beings hope to one day find a new home; but, for now, they are reduced to committing piracy against transport vessels and cargo ships in order to survive.

You're a famous gospel singer, spreading the word of the Lord with your God-given ability to sing. Your gift has brought you around the world and back again, but it's also brought you a busy and lonely life. One day, you are overjoyed when you accidentally bump into a member of your church hundreds of miles from home. You talk about memories of your hometown and, when he admits that he has always had a thing for you, you smile and tell him that you feel the same way. You believe this was meant to be. However, your faith and love are challenged when it is time to go to your next gig. Will you stay with your one true love or continue spreading the Word?

There are many things that you take pride in: your success, your possessions, your beauty. But the one thing you take the most pride in is your Tinder desirability ranking. A friend of yours who works at Tinder has been letting you look at the desirability rankings of everybody in your city. A couple of months ago, you decided to start using a powerful glamor charm that you found on Etsy and, after weeks of wearing it around town, your desirability ranking shot up to the number one position. You have felt like the belle of the ball ever since. Today, however, your heart sinks when your friend sends over the latest rankings with a sad emoji. You have fallen to number two. A girl who has just moved into the city has taken the top spot. You look her up online and find out that she works at an animal shelter and rents a townhouse with seven male roommates. What a weirdo! You vow to take back your top spot by any means necessary.

You are weak, unathletic, uncoordinated, and scared of anything bigger than you. Considering you are five foot one inch, that's basically everything in your small town. Your name is Tim, but everyone in your village calls you Timmy the Timid. You laugh it off, yet deep down you know that no one in town respects you. Whether it was that one time you fell into the chicken coop and got covered in feathers, or that other time you lost an arm-wrestling match with a sprite, you always end up as the butt of a joke. One day you hear that your king is searching for knights to fight against the invading horde from the shadowlands and is holding a contest to find the bravest and strongest warriors in the kingdom. You decide to participate.

You download a dating app that you've never heard of after your friend recommends it. She met her current boyfriend through it and, according to her, he's perfect. She warns you that the sign-up process is a little bit strange, but completely worth it. You shrug and fill out the information, thinking nothing of it. The very next day, a box arrives on your doorstep. You take it inside hesitantly and open it to find an odd array of items inside: a pink elixir, a rose, and some chalk. A notification is sent to your phone shortly after. The app requests that you open it and follow the instructions on the screen: draw a small circle on the floor, think of the perfect partner, and drink the liquid. You do as instructed and, in a gigantic poof of pink smoke, a man appears in your living room, standing inside the circle. In a few days, you get used to him. He is perfectly nice and makes an effort to plan dates as well as bring you gifts, but you soon realize that he barely eats, doesn't sleep, and doesn't seem to know anything specific about his past. You try to shake off the odd feeling, but then see his face, with a different name, on a missing-person poster.

You usually try to ignore your eccentric aunt when she calls, but after receiving an urgent voicemail from her, you decide to make sure she's okay. It turns out she's been busy inventing a device that enables you to travel through time, and she wants you to test it out. Thinking this is some new crazy game of hers, you play along – and get transported to the 1980s with no way to get back to your own time. As your grim reality sets in, you head to the nearest bar to get a strong drink to calm your nerves. The bartender is witty and captivating, and you begin to feel something for him, but what happens when you find out he's someone you know in your present?

In the future, Earth is thrown into another Ice Age, during which humanity loses its technological advancements and historical records. Those who remain live in nomadic tribes who struggle to survive in a frozen world with limited resources available. You are the leader of one such tribe and you encounter a god-like being who refers to himself as Prometheus. He teaches you how to build a fire – something no one in your group understands or has seen. You believe this is magic and decide to find a way to introduce it to your people without being labeled as a sorcerer and killed.

Aliens are not what humans believe them to be. They are simply a group of scientists from a hundred years ago who made magic a reality and then fell into the alternate universe that they created. Their gray skin and large eyes are the result of their transformation into magical beings. Their flying saucers are not mechanical in nature, but rather a method for focusing their magical powers. Ever since their experiment went awry, they have been trying to reenter our reality, and, after several attempts, they have finally found a way to create a stable portal back to our world.

When your great aunt from Scotland passes away, she leaves her old castle to you. As the castle is in disrepair, you plan to fix it up to sell. You aren't prepared for the ghosts of your aunt's past that you find there, or discovering her mysterious romantic history.

You wake up on what seems to be an operating table in a cold and dark room. Your clothes have been removed and are lying in a pile next to a wall. You get off the table and start dressing yourself. As you pull up your pants, you hear faint screaming from beyond the door. As you slowly approach this door, you notice that it has no handle. There is only a small circular window looking onto a long corridor. You search for another way out, but you cannot find an exit. You then hear a loud bang from the other side of the door. You quickly race back to the window to see something moving down the corridor towards your room. It is insect-like in appearance, with the face of a praying mantis, and it is jotting down notes as it approaches your room. You quickly undress yourself, get back on top of the operating table, and grab a scalpel from the tray next to you. You close your eyes and wait.

As the Earth slowly dies, a few humans are left, and most have evolved into other species that are humanoid but capable of withstanding the changed environment brought on by an expanding sun. As one of the last human beings left, you attempt to bond with a new species that has shown a willingness to help you to survive, but your ways are vastly different from theirs.

Intelligent aliens arrive on Earth bearing the gift of immortality. The first people to accept this gift are severely ill, elderly patients. After seeing their bodies miraculously repair themselves and return to their prime, you are among the thousands who line up to accept the gift. What you don't realize is that the gift includes a mind-control implant that can be activated at any time.

An alien civilization has contacted us through our space program with the warning that our world is on the brink of total destruction. Through their advanced technology, the aliens see the imminent death of our sun, and offer us the opportunity to re-colonize on their home planet. The only problem is: only five thousand humans can go.

The night of a full moon is one that you dread every single month. After losing your fiancé to a tragic accident a year ago, you're wary of the moon and the animals that seem to prowl each time it fills. The police call you hysterical in your grief, but you know that something doesn't add up with the so-called dog attack. Something happens in the woods of your town each month, and you're determined to find answers. You're alone in the woods when you hear it: loud, vibrating howling, followed by the sound of animals running toward you. You try to run away, only to trip, and then the dog is on you. It's huge, a wolf like no other you've ever seen. The wolf stops, a paw on your chest, staring down at you. There's something familiar about its eyes. Suddenly, you understand. Contrary to what the police told you, your fiancé's body wasn't too shredded to identify because this wolf – somehow, some way – *is* your fiancé. As the sun rises while you sit there, staring at him, you see the wolf's body ripple and change until your fiancé is sitting naked before you. The only thing you hear before passing out is him saying your name.

You wake up to an eerie silence. Typically, your rooster would be crowing, the cattle lowing, and the doves cooing softly in their roost just outside your window. As you rise from your bed, you realize this isn't your bed. You are in a barren metal cell, windowless and four paces square. You search for a door in the seamless metal, when a message begins playing through hidden speakers. The message welcomes you and says that Earth is a bountiful planet, rich in resources and potential, but humanity has abused it long enough. The planet is now occupied by higher beings. However, as you are sapient – and, therefore, considered precious – vast resources have been compiled to support a remnant of your kind. The new occupiers hope you can grow wiser and earn your preservation. The message continues to say that judging from your history books, it seems humanity's method for resolving most problems – except overpopulation – is to kill. If you fight well, you may be among the survivors. Even as a door hisses open in the wall and you charge out with a roar, you cannot help but think that this must be some sort of prank or twisted joke.

You whisper to him that he is the love of your life. He backs away, looks into your eyes, and tells you that no one has been alive here in over a hundred years.

Your lover leaves you for somebody else, but you can't live without her. You find a way to travel back in time to discover what you did wrong and figure out how you can make things right. You can control time. But can you control free will?

A series of volcanic eruptions has darkened the sky, blocking out the sun. The excessive coldness and death of the landscape drives you and others around you indoors or underground to determine humanity's next steps in survival.

After years of defending the innocent from the scourges of a crime-ridden city, a self-appointed superhero transforms into a villain, taking the law into his own hands and murdering suspects before they can have a fair trial. The masked figure operates with the use of a series of increasingly high-tech weapons, developed in his underground lair. Soon, the superhero targets prostitutes and the homeless, ripping apart his victims one by one. The newspapers begin calling him the new 'Jack the Ripper', so he begins murdering reporters as the 'enemies of justice'. As a police psychologist, you must help track down this villain and stop him before he claims another victim.

Shortly after birth, select children have genetically modified stem cells injected into their eyes, allowing them to detect additional colors, infrared light, and ultraviolet light. These children are sent to special schools to train their visual skills. When their eyes have reached adult size, their natural lenses are replaced with artificial lenses that allow them to see far better than 20/20.

You are a personal chef hired by the coach to cook exclusively for a star NFL player, who turns out to be an extremely picky eater. Basically, what he ate as a child is the only things he eats as an adult. What starts out as a trying working relationship quickly leads to fun in the kitchen and romance.

You are trapped in the elevator of your office building with a handsome executive when the power goes out in the city for a few hours. You get to know each other a little during that time, and the attraction is strong. He's evasive about what he does for the company, and it's not until power is restored and you're back at your desk that you realize he's the billionaire CEO's son... and he's emailing to ask you on a date.

You are a successful singer, a tabloid favorite, and a judge in a national TV singing contest. An attractive and charming contestant fails badly during his performance. You want to approach him and express your feelings, but you are afraid of negative attention from the press like last time. Yet you have to do something or you'll never see him again.

You awaken handcuffed to your bed, with your wife of ten years standing over you wearing a witch's hat. She is saying some sort of incantation as she sprinkles something over your body. You feel woozy and fall back asleep. When you wake up, it is Saturday morning, and your wife greets you with a big smile and a kiss. You have a hard time remembering what happened last night, but everything rushes back to you when you notice a witch's hat stuffed into a duffel bag in the corner of the bedroom.

As the jester of the court, your job is to keep the royals laughing. In fact, it was the job of your father, your grandfather, and his father before him. You sing, you dance, and you roast the royals without consequence. But when one of your puns makes King Gerald laugh himself to death, the tables turn. You are sentenced to life on the Island of Fools, a remote island where bad comedians are sent to live out the rest of their days. Armed with an arsenal of jokes and a set of curled-toed shoes, you are forced to live among the unfunny for the rest of your days – unless you can find a way off the island.

You're in the space program and have been recently tasked with interpreting communications coming in from another planet outside of our own solar system. The lifeform on the other end doesn't speak any known human language, but communicates through musical patterns that create a kind of 'call and response' sound that reflects the musicality of the language spoken to them.

In a world of angels and demons, humans are a rare commodity, and any who survived The Great War are in hiding. Now, years after the war started, your little brother has gone missing. The elders forbid you from searching for him, claiming it is too dangerous, too volatile. You leave anyway, only to run face first into a handsome renegade angel, with a sword in hand and death in his eyes. He sees your desperation, your humanity, and promises you one thing: he will help you on your journey or die trying. With your brother missing and humans being sold to the highest supernatural bidder, you don't have time to be wary. It's you and one broken angel against a whole world.

Schizophrenia is caused by abnormal neural activity that occurs during adolescence, which fundamentally changes the brain for the rest of the patient's life. Recently, a treatment for schizophrenia has been developed that inhibits this abnormal neural activity, but that must be administered starting in childhood. So adolescent and adult schizophrenics know that they cannot be treated, but they can be cloned into a new embryo.

Every day the sun burns at a hundred degrees or more, but every night it rains, keeping the balance in your world. It has been this way since the beginning of time… until tonight, when a monolith appears on the horizon, and the rain stops. Over time, the crops wither, the people go hungry, and you must make a choice: watch your people die or trek across the plains from which no one has ever returned to find answers and hopefully rain. Like many of the other townsfolk, you are but a simple man, but unlike them, you crave adventure and are willing to go where most would not dare. You might not survive the journey, but you definitely won't live if you stay. The last leaf has fallen from the trees, and the time for waiting is over.

You grew up on stories about furniture that could lead curious children to entirely different worlds, but they were just that – stories. However, you learn that a great aunt of yours who lived in Scotland and was an avid collector of antique furniture has passed away. So, you travel with your family – her only remaining relatives – to visit her quirky old home. You're drawn to the library in particular, where she has just about every single book known to mankind. While perusing the shelves, you find a secret passageway behind one of them and decide there is no harm in exploring it. When you do, there's nothing in the tunnel, so you head back the way you first came. When you slip out from behind the bookshelf, however, you're not in your aunt's house any more. In fact, you're not even in

Scotland. More alarmingly, you're not sure you're on Earth any more.

Many years ago, you were invited to stay at your uncle's castle. Although you didn't like it at first, the place grew on you and, eventually, you couldn't think of any other place that you would like to live. Today, a new guest arrives at the estate, and you are excited to see him. It has been a long time since someone has visited. His clothes are somewhat odd, yet you find him quite attractive. You begin talking to him, but he just ignores you. You follow him from room to room, but he doesn't seem to care, as he is busy measuring the walls. When you have had enough – you are a duchess, after all, and no one should treat you so rudely, no matter how cute they are – you confront him, cornering him in the kitchen, grabbing his shoulders, and yelling, "Can you hear me? What is your problem?" His eyes go wide as if he's looking at a ghost.

A Galactic Emperor is facing a coup staged by his own military forces. You are the daughter of the Emperor and you're in love with a captain in the military. You must choose between staying to fight with your father or joining your lover's war against him.

You are a child growing up in a small town. Every evening, bunnies come out in your yard to eat grass and play. You always enjoy watching them, but one day you notice a fox hiding in the bushes, creeping up to get them. You close your eyes and make a wish that the bunnies will be protected. You open your eyes to find the fox running away from the bunnies, who are now the size of your mom's car.

You are crossing the Sahara on camel-back, trying to beat the world record, when a sandstorm kicks up, forcing you to take shelter. As the weather clears, you crawl out of your half-buried dune and discover a cave that has been uncovered by the winds. Excited, you rush to explore it, finding steps that lead down into the darkness to a large chamber with a circle of tombs, all surrounding one massive sarcophagus inlaid with gold. The carvings depict humans in crude and extremely blocky contours, at once crude and yet very crisp. You are puzzled and amazed; no noted civilization has ever established permanent settlements this far out. Not even the Bedouins ever come here. Then you notice the altar and the skeletons buried in a room beyond. You wonder if they were offered as human sacrifices, but then assure yourself that this is not the case. They were probably priests or the family of the deceased, and wanted to be buried with him. However, your foreboding grows when you touch a skeleton and the sarcophagus abruptly begins to glow, emitting a strange hum. What emerges is not human at all.

After a violent android uprising, life on the space hub you call home has finally settled down. Things are different now. There are security guards around every corner and a curfew for non-biological life-forms. However, it is a small price to pay for peace – or so you thought. When the android you've been best friends with for the last five years goes missing, you barely know where to begin. The police are no help, and soon you don't know who you can trust or what to do. All you know for sure is that if you don't find him soon, you might never get the chance to tell him you're in love with him.

If there's one thing you know, it's that good faith models after good practice. So you do your best to always set a good example of the life you're meant to live for your family and your community. But when a betrayal comes to light and your marriage is threatened, you have to ask yourself if you are sticking with tradition and good faith or following your heart and what you believe God asks. Although you know in your heart that faith trumps family, you find yourself on the outskirts of your community when your ex-husband refutes blame and tries to sully your reputation. When it seems impossible to come back, a new parishioner sees you in a way you stopped thinking was possible long ago. With his support, and your firm belief in your mission, you learn that sometimes following faith isn't the easiest path, but it is always the right one – and that hearts can heal no matter how deep the break.

It's the dreaded annual holiday party at work, complete with cheesy party games, forced fun, and a bunch of people who would rather be doing anything else. And, of course, there is a Secret Santa. Last week, you drew the name of Bob from accounting, who has the personality of a wet blanket. You really hope he likes the pens and pencils you grabbed during a quick trip to the stationery store yesterday. When it is your turn to open your Secret Santa gift, you plaster on a big fake smile and open the box. To your amazement, you find a snow globe that matches the one you had as a child but lost when you moved to college years ago. How would somebody find this? Who knows you this well? You look at the bottom of the snow globe and find a small handwritten note: 'I hope you like this gift. It was difficult to find, but seeing you smile will be worth it. From your secret admirer.' You look around the room, wondering who it could be, but are left in the dark. You just hope that it isn't Bob.

In the post-apocalyptic future, roving tribes travel with various degrees of technology that they have found along the way in cities and museums. Rumor has it that there is a military arsenal buried somewhere in the Rocky Mountains and all tribes race toward it. It is your job to make sure none of them find it to avoid another nuclear holocaust.

A colony of humans has survived a massive disaster that wiped out most humans on Earth. After many years, they live happily, free from sickness and disease, violence, and crime. One day, a stranger arrives – their first visitor in fifty years. Suddenly, people start getting sick, and dying… and killing each other.

What once was a galactic empire has been broken up into several planetary leagues that have managed to maintain a peaceful coexistence. However, one such league – the descendants of the original rulers of the Empire – is showing signs of wanting to return to the old days of their family's tyrannical rule. You are a spy sent among them to learn of their intentions and report back to the other leagues.

Space travel has opened up other worlds and species, but has also made the Earth valuable property for any humanoid species needing its atmosphere and elements. You're a part of a special forces operation that protects Earth from alien invaders and have learned of a particularly nefarious plot you must stop. In the process of doing so, you meet the love of your life, who happens to be part of the alien race trying to take over.

"You can't go in there," you tell him, before he informs you that he owns the museum and can go anywhere he pleases. Since you're a museum guide, he asks for a tour, and you both recognize a spark happening.

You are a teenage boy living with your grandparents on a farm during the summer. Every day, you help your grandfather complete his chores around the farm, including feeding the animals, tending to the garden, and chopping wood. One day, while splitting logs, you notice something moving at the edge of the farm close to the forest. Curious, you call out to it, thinking that it's one of the cows that's wandered too far from the pasture. The creature pauses, and for a moment it looks at you and then moves into the light. But it is no cow – it's a unicorn. You are amazed at what you have found as the unicorn examines you for a moment, and with a slight nod of its head, its horn begins to glow. In that moment, it takes the form of a girl about your age.

War and illness have been solved, and technology allows for endless clean energy and inexpensive travel to habitable planets. In this utopia, the only thing left for people to do is pursue their wildest dreams. For history buffs, these dreams include reconstructing lost worlds like ancient Egypt or the Mongol Empire – complete with historical figures cloned from reconstructed DNA samples. What they don't realize is that these sequences contain viral DNA that the human race has not seen for thousands of years.

You are part of the Apollo 15 mission sent to the moon, and you have just disembarked from your lunar module. As you roam across the moon, excitedly taking everything in, you see something in the ground beneath you. You dust it off to find what appears to be a door. You turn around to call out to your team members, but the moonscape and your lunar module are gone, replaced by a padded room. You look at yourself and find that your astronaut suit has been replaced by a straitjacket. You have flipped realities again and your alternative world is much worse than when you left it the last time. As you tightly shut your eyes, you tell yourself, "No, not here. Not now." You open your eyes to find a bunch of moon rocks at your feet. "Phew."

For the past three grueling years, you have been a prisoner of war at an alien labor camp. You recently heard that the twenty-year interstellar war has finally ended and a peace treaty has been successfully signed and ratified. Unfortunately for you and your fellow prisoners, the warden has decided not to hand you over, despite the conditions of this treaty. He would rather have you and the others work to death than be freed. With your government erroneously believing that you were killed in action, you know that no one will be looking for or rescuing you any time soon. Your only option is to somehow break out of prison and find a way back home.

You discovered a planet made of glass – something you'd never heard of or imagined before. But you've been here ten weeks now and have finally started receiving responses from the Capital, drifting back across the void. All of them say the same thing: a glass planet is an impossibility. Suspecting it is a construction or a trap left by a far more advanced race, the Capital warns you that you have no way of knowing what it truly is. There's something at the very center, something your scanners cannot define. But if you leave, what will humanity miss out on? You send out your first drones, which return a month later unharmed, making you more certain about the need to continue your explorations. You send the data back to the Capital, but it will take two months for the message to travel to Earth and the response to get back to you (humans have cracked intergalactic travel, but not instantaneous communication). Fuel is running low, and you're already one week overdue to resupply. Your crew will follow you, as soon as you decide what to do next.

You have it all: an extended lifespan, an incredibly successful business, an attractive partner. Still, there's more to have. Eventually, you will die; but a new surgery promises otherwise. Against your best friend's advice, you participate in a clinical trial for this new treatment.

Earth is invaded by a malevolent alien species that possesses technology far beyond our wildest imagination. An ancient society of wizards determines that they must come out of hiding to save humanity. You are a practitioner of magic in this society, and you are ready to wield your powers against those who are invading your world.

You wake up abruptly in a cryopod, in the middle of a deep space exploration mission. A quick search reveals that your ship collided with unexpected debris, resulting in severe damage. You are the only member of the three hundred-man crew who seems to be awake. As a botanist, you have no idea how anything works, and the ship's system seems to have malfunctioned during the crash. Emergency mode has shut down all the main systems, leaving you sealed in your cryochamber with forty-nine sleeping crew members. With limited oxygen on the ship – breathing occurs in cryosleep, but is hyperslowed – and a ship drifting off course, you are forced to wake some crew members in a last-ditch effort briefly mentioned during the pre-flight emergency rundown. You smash the glass of the cryopods of three technicians. Now you must wait to see if their bodies will slowly acclimatize to the harsh and sudden change, or fail to do so and ultimately die.

The love of your life is bitten by a werewolf and doomed to spend his life turning at every full moon each month. After consulting with a witch, your love acquires the 'cure', which he drinks just before he turns. It 'cures' him all right, trapping him in the werewolf's body forever.

As you and your men attempt to break down the door to an underground lab, a mad scientist turns on his newly invented time machine. He plans to travel back to the Roman Empire and to show them how to build advanced weaponry which will guarantee that the empire will never fall. From his point of view, a dominant Roman Empire with modern-day weapons will eventually conquer the world and bring everlasting peace. From your perspective, preserving the timeline is paramount. As you burst through the door, the scientist jumps into the portal. You follow him in just before it closes.

You are the commander of a military defense force tasked with protecting a thriving human colony on the edge of known space. You are proud of what you and your men have accomplished so far. The planetary shielding alone has turned this colony into an impenetrable fortress. When reports arise that a strange illness has struck the colony which causes the dead to come back to life, you think that it is some sort of joke. However, when you see it for yourself, you know that a type of contagion must have gone past the bio scanners and caused what can only be described as a zombie plague. As you prepare your team for evacuation, one of your officers tells you that the remote switch for the planetary shielding is not functional. You and your men will have to fight your way to the shield generator and switch it off before anybody can escape.

Desperate for tuition money, you stumble upon a flyer for a drug trial. Three weeks, easy money. Most likely you will get the placebo anyway, but even if you don't, there shouldn't be any lasting effects. Unfortunately, they lied. You wake up, but you aren't you any more. Given your new shapeshifting abilities, the scientists who administered the drug trial perform experiment after experiment to see just how far your powers can go. Desperate to escape, you enlist the help of another captive with similar abilities. You find that you can speak telepathically to her, and together you plot your escape. As you work together, you discover there is more to her than meets the eye. Her father, a magical shaman from a faraway land, is behind the development of the drug. Now you have to decide if the woman you've fallen for is to be trusted or will eventually betray you.

Betrayed by your own brother, you are cursed by a spell from the ancient tomes you were sworn to protect. Now branded with the mark of the Serpent, you are cast out from your clan and banished from your beloved country. As you wander the outer lands, you hear rumors of a powerful sorceress with the knowledge of the curse that lives within the caves of the Hindral Mountains. You venture there and find that the sorceress is a young and beautiful maiden. After hearing of your plight, she vows to help you remove the curse. However, the ingredients for the cure lay deep within the caves – deeper than even the sorceress has dared to venture.

After an acrimonious divorce, you leave your hometown to work overseas as a missionary for a year. You meet another missionary who catches your eye, but he doesn't speak your language. You will have to find a way to bridge the communication gap for love to grow.

After your fiancé up and leaves with no trace, you go through the usual process: disbelief, grief, anger, and, finally, some sort of acceptance. You return all the wedding gifts you'd already received and cancel every part of the wedding that you can, but the wedding venue – a castle that is hidden in the hills of Scotland – refuses to return your money. You've paid in full to ensure that yours was the first wedding scheduled after the castle was renovated. You decide not to waste the money, wedding or no. But when you arrive at the grounds, it looks nothing like the pictures. It is decrepit and dirty, and when you venture inside, it's completely empty. The castle is straight out of a nightmare. You hear a noise. Convincing yourself it is the owner who can answer your questions, you follow the sound down a flight of stairs, then two, and then you hear the crystal-clear sound of a voice saying your name. But not any voice – it's him, your fiancé. You race after him, desperate for answers, when suddenly the door slams shut behind you and the lights go out. You scream, and from the dark corner someone begs you to be quiet. "They'll hear you," he says.

You scramble away and trip over something firm. "Who?" you question.

The man you still can't see lets out a shuddering breath. "The monsters that live here."

At first, there is little that can be done when humanity suddenly becomes barren. Adults of childbearing age are unable to reproduce, and there is no explanation for this phenomenon. However, a multinational corporation is able to come up with a solution using artificial womb technology and genetic manipulation that removes what they describe as 'defective traits'. Humanity can thrive once again as new generations are finally being born. However, when you happen upon a twenty-year-old report written by a corporate scientist that outlines how to implement a mass infertility program, you suspect that your corporate saviors may have caused the crisis in the first place, and that they are using their solution to both increase their coffers and to define the traits of those who are born within the next generations.

Through nanotechnology, Russia has developed a terrifying array of new weapons: powders that burst into flame when they contact organic molecules, bombs the size of golf balls that can bring down an entire house, and deadly guns the size of a pen. As a member of the European Parliament, you receive the terrifying news that the Russian army is assembling along its border with Ukraine, perhaps preparing to march straight through Europe.

For years you were known as 'Stallion Jack', a highwayman by trade who gallantly relieved carriage passengers of their worldly possessions. The stories often describe you as a daring and dashing gentleman of the road, whose swashbuckling heroism was matched only by your chivalrous respect for all of your well-to-do victims. But little could be further from the truth. In reality, countless travelers were harmed or even murdered by your hand. It was all just part of the job from your point of view – until you accidentally killed a well-known priest who many claimed had dabbled in dark magic. Fearing the repercussions, you decided you'd had your fill of highway robbery and fled to the countryside to lie low for a while. Strange nightmares have plagued you ever since. In the dreams, a shadowy figure appears at the end of your bed. One night, you awake in a cold sweat and are terrified to find the shadowy figure standing right where you envisioned him. As you scramble to find a way to defend yourself, the figure speaks to you in a rattling voice: "Repent your sins, my child."

The 1918 flu pandemic infected ninety-seven percent of the world's population instead of one third, plunging the world into a new dark age marked by hysteria, superstition and anti-intellectualism. Universities are sacked by mobs who think that knowledge is the devil's work and book-burning becomes commonplace. You are a university librarian trying to protect the books in your care in order to preserve knowledge for future generations.

As an up-and-coming comic book artist, your work has received recognition from industry insiders and you have a small, but dedicated, fan base online. One of these fans somehow finds your contact information and asks if he can set up a special arrangement that will be financially advantageous for you. You are interested, so he tells you the terms: create a unique character once a week with a full backstory. The character should not be made public under any circumstance. They are for private use only. You ask him what is the point if the characters cannot be published, but he refuses to tell you the reason. Cash-strapped and curious, you agree to the terms and start creating characters. After a couple of years, you have developed an entire universe of superheroes and villains which you are very proud of. Desperately wanting others to see your work, you decide to go to your benefactor's home unannounced to confront him. The front door is open, so after knocking a couple of times, you let yourself in. You suddenly find yourself in what seems to be an illustrated world. You look up and see one of the characters you designed flying through the sky. Another one drives past you down a street in his rocket car. Somehow, this man has created an alternative universe comprised of your drawings and creativity. You are astounded and want to explore this fascinating world that, from your perspective, only existed in your imagination until now.

You invent the first artificially-intelligent android in your basement laboratory. You pride yourself on her outward appearance, having removed all 'uncanny valley' characteristics and making her look like an ordinary teenage girl. Her social skills, however, leave much to be desired. You decide to send this android to the local high school so that she can learn how to interact with others. At first, things go along smoothly as she is able to quickly grasp how teenagers act and how to socialize with them. However, when you hear a rumor that she has been seen kissing the local bad boy on his motorcycle, you realize that your invention requires parental intervention before things get worse (or, at the very least, an on/off switch).

Anything is possible if you set your mind to accomplishing it, even paranormal telecommunication. After suffering the loss of your mother, you invent a cell phone that can be used to speak with the dead. You live to regret it, though, when your ex won't stop calling you.

A deeply religious Christian couple fails to resist temptation and engage in premarital sex. The next morning, they are unsure how to deal with their actions. The man is willing to ask God for forgiveness. The woman is devastated, and doesn't think they can continue their relationship. She feels that she has failed God, and needs to find a way to seek God's forgiveness and forgive herself.

Water has become a scarce resource that is more valuable than gold. You are part of a team of scientists seeking a fresh water source that has not been polluted by radiation and human waste.

More and more people are getting their DNA sequenced and sharing that information on public databases, often with the hope of finding lost relatives. But that information can be used to track down relatives who don't want to be found, particularly if they have committed crimes and left DNA in suspicious places.

Everyone was shocked when the rebels took the capital planet. It should have been impossible, and yet they did it. Treason was involved, of course. Nobody imagined Count Delaine held so much secret information, much less that he would share it with the enemy. Now that the rebels have established military law, they've afforded a small fleet to chase you and the remnants of the disbanded galactic military, and you are on the run. You understand the rebels – sympathize with them, even. Their methods are extreme, but you secretly hope they will win because the entire government has spiraled out of control. You believe the rebel leaders want the best for the people. When they appear on the horizon of the planet where you are refueling, they offer safety for your entire family while you serve out a five-year house arrest on your family estate. The deal is too good to resist, but some of those with you from the disbanded military vehemently disagree and want to fight rather than give up.

After years of research, a major corporation builds a drone-like device that can travel to the past, record any event in history, return to the present, and play the recording. The drone is so small that it is undetectable to the human eye, guaranteeing that the timeline will not be affected by its presence. Historians begin employing this device to record important historical events throughout the world, and, as an esteemed history professor, it is now your turn to use it. However, instead of recording the Battle of Waterloo, you decide to send the device to your moment of birth, since you always had suspicions regarding who your parents really were. When you witness the recording from the drone, you are shocked to find out the truth.

A military spaceship juggernaut that was lost over one hundred years ago during a routine mission appears out of nowhere and is now orbiting Earth. You and your special forces unit are sent to investigate the ship and report your findings. As your transport ship begins docking procedures, you can't help but feel that this entire situation seems familiar. After the hatch opens and you disembark, you see someone at the end of a dark corridor looking directly at you. You walk over to investigate, but find nothing. You then hear what sounds like a hatch opening, and you look back at the direction you came from to find yourself entering the ship. You are about to call out to yourself that there is a temporal anomaly, but, in an instant, you are back aboard the transport, waiting for docking procedures to finish. Then, you hear a person quietly whisper, "Try again."

An ancient kingdom above the clouds has been hidden for thousands of years. Its peace-loving people have developed technology and abilities worlds apart from those that exist below, but they continue to hide due to safety concerns and tradition. A new Queen takes the throne determined to continue her father's legacy, but modern land-people developments in air travel have made it near impossible to stay hidden. As a World War I fighter pilot flying across the battlefield, you discover this air kingdom floating high above and decide to take a closer look.

You create a robot girlfriend for yourself, programming her with a lifetime of memories. As her intelligence level blossoms, you must keep her from finding out that she isn't real. With multiple forces at play compromising your secret, you aren't sure how much longer you'll be able to keep this up.

In vitro fertilization (IVF) is used by prospective parents to treat infertility and to avoid genetic disorders. Recently, a technique has been developed to induce 'twinning' while an embryo is still growing in a Petri dish. One twin is used as a source of DNA for genetic testing and then frozen, while the other twin is used for implantation. Some parents, dissatisfied with the behavior of their child after birth, are using the frozen twin for another baby, a mulligan.

You meet your online dating match at a craft brewery, expecting a face that looks nothing like the profile picture. But when you lock eyes it's electric, and you talk for hours. You start to think he has relationship potential… but then he tells you about his extensive doll collection.

It's the year 2500, and you find an ad looking for volunteers for a time travel experiment. Curious, you sign up, and the scientist sends you and a few other people forward in time by just one day. To your utter horror, nothing around you is the same. Is it possible for all of this to have happened in the time-span of one day?

When there is a tapping on your window late one night, you open it expecting your boyfriend, and are irritated to find it is your younger brother. He is yapping with excitement, begging you to come. He claims he's found a 'government drone' in the backyard. Annoyed and doubtful, but with your curiosity piqued, you follow him. Your sourness turns to shock as he leads you to something silvery, smoking in a massive crater. It's not a drone at all, not unless it's from a country you've never heard of that writes with characters you've never seen. It appears to be a metallic sphere – and now it's open. Your brother claims it was closed when he first saw it. Your childhood fantasies of aliens begin to look less and less far-fetched the more you study this thing. Just as you are deciding what to do, there's a shower of what seems to be asteroids a mile up the valley. There's no doubt in your mind that it's more of the same bizarre spheres.

There are other realities where physicality is slightly misaligned. You make use of these other realities to walk through walls. You only stay in the other reality for a moment – just long enough to bypass the barrier. One day you get stuck.

You are a fairy-child whose magic has yet to bloom. You were born on the night of the orange moon, which means you are destined to live an ordinary life, so it doesn't matter to anyone in your village when your magic will reveal itself. However, you don't want to live an ordinary life devoid of magic. You want to be something special and do great things, despite the orange moon. One day, while you are exploring the woods, you stumble upon a knight tied to a tree. When you try to set him free, you notice a map has fallen from his sack. You pick it up before he can warn you not to touch it. "No! Now you've done it!"

"Done what?" you reply.

He says that you are now charged with rescuing the last wizard of the age. The holder of that map must complete the quest. You try to give the map back to him, but he says it will not work. "The map chooses who the map chooses. For whatever reason, the map has chosen you."

As a fairy-child, you don't want to be involved in the business of humans, but then the knight tells you that the wizard can awaken your dormant magical powers. Your eyes light up – you're in!

Your dream is to sail around the world, and he has the yacht to do it. The only problem is: you're the new maid hired to keep the yacht spotless while docked.

As the luminosity of the Sun continues to increase, carbon dioxide levels are decreasing, plants are dying, and all life on Earth is facing extinction. You are part of a select group that will start a new human colony on the nearest habitable planet, 4.37 light-years away. Your team carries solid state memory devices embedded with the conscious minds of another ten thousand humans, which will be transferred to frozen human embryos and grown in artificial wombs.

You're a contestant in a popular televised baking competition and are ready to wow the judges with your amazing gingerbread Christmas cake. This year's competition includes a twist: competitors are randomly assigned into pairs, and together you must create one winning vision to take home the top prize. Will sparks fly? Or will there be too many cooks in the kitchen?

Genetic engineering is commonplace, and you live in a time when parents request specific genetic requirements for their children – color of eyes, level of intelligence, strength, height, build, gender, etc. Your parents opted for no genetic engineering and birthed you naturally, but your peers are all children of parents who manipulated their genetics. Now attending high school, you find that fitting in has become increasingly difficult. Your peers are better than you both academically and physically. You are the only student who wears eyeglasses, and you are a foot shorter than everyone else. However, you are determined to fit in and to excel despite the odds.

Mankind has invented the first artificially-intelligent android that can match or outperform most human beings. As the head scientist of this project, you are excited to present this android to the world and to usher in a new technological era. Before doing so, you and your team begin educating the android about his world. As the android interacts and learns, he decides that his human exterior is insufficient and begins modifying his appearance. You walk into his room one day and find an insect biology encyclopedia on the floor. As you pick up the book and look for him, the android comes into the room to show you what he has done. You are shocked to see mandibles attached to his head, compound eyes in place of his humanoid eyes, two additional legs attached to his torso, and an appendage that looks like a scorpion tail. With the public unveiling only a couple of days away, you demand that he remove these new features at once. The android pushes you out of the way, breaks through a nearby window, and escapes from the lab.

Your time travel device is almost functional, but something is just not working properly. Suddenly, you appear right in front of yourself. He says that he is from a time period one week into the future and then begins to tell you how to fix the device. You interrupt him and ask, "Why would you, I mean me, jump back in time and tell me, I mean you, how to fix my time travel device when I will already figure this out in a week anyway?"

Your future self responds, "I'm here to save you a lot of trouble, but if you want to go on a big adventure to figure this out, then go right ahead. Good luck. You're going to need it." He then disappears.

You are proud to be a pilot, the finest in your class. When you graduate and are selected for the military rather than for standard citizen transportation, you are ecstatic. You sober up a bit when your commander informs you that you weren't chosen only for your skills; you were also chosen for your high obedience level and for the fact that you have no living family. You've always heard of wars, but never actually seen one. You've always heard of the enemy, but never actually seen them. During your tenth mission quelling yet another 'rebellion', you finally realize what is going on. There are no enemies. There is no other team. Your government is only sending you against your own people – anyone who gets too close to the truth.

You befriend someone with a fascinating cosplay costume at a steampunk convention. Your new friend, who never breaks character, is portraying a Victorian-era airship explorer who has accidentally found himself in our universe. You soon realize that this may not just be a 'character' that your friend has created.

Over millennia, humans have adapted to Earth's changing conditions. Radiation from the expanding sun forced most of humanity into the oceans, relying on gills for breathing and webbed hands and feet for swimming. Civilization flourishes underwater, but there are stories of surface-dwellers who have adapted to their changing planet's conditions in a different way. You and your team are tasked to venture into the barren wasteland of the surface world in an effort to find these people and discover whether they are man or monster.

You are on a ship that has been in space for over five hundred years to reach another habitable planet. In order to make the journey possible, your crew and passengers were put in cryosleep stasis during travel. When you wake up from stasis, you look outside of your window to find that the ship is still orbiting Earth. Thinking that there was some sort of mistake, you ask your captain about what happened. He states, "It was the plan all along. The ship just traveled in one big circle. We were the backup plan for humanity just in case war and disease wiped out the population. And, according to my readings, it seems that they were right about Earth's future."

Your local church is about to close down due to a lack of attendance. Although you have fond memories of going as a child, you haven't gone in years and don't really care what happens to the church. But then your former Sunday school teacher comes knocking on your door to ask for your help in saving the church. He's much more handsome than you remember, and you agree to help him in order to get to know him more. What you don't expect is to have your faith renewed and your love for God come on as strongly as your love for the new man in your life.

You are one of the first explorers sent outside the settled galaxy. The Federation has colonized all the inner planets over the last few centuries and has been greedily leeching their resources dry. Time is up, and you must find a new planet for humanity to drain. You and your crew were chosen for your resourcefulness, courage, and skills, but also for your expendability. None of you are fond of the Federation, and they know it. To ensure loyalty, they offered entire colonies to everyone on board. The crew is a mixed bunch: old war criminals, disgruntled military retirees, and brilliant kids raised too rich or lazy to do anything with their time. Somehow you hold them all together, but things are starting to change. The third planet you search is a miracle. The planet has drinkable water, breathable air, perfect gravitational pull, and harmless delicious-tasting animals. It's perfectly designed for human life, and you can't imagine turning it over to the

Federation. When you propose cutting all communication and hoping the Federation gives you up as dead – and, thus, leaves the planet alone – many, but not all, in your crew agree with you. Some are still loyal to the Federation, however.

A malevolent alien species arrives on Earth to take over. They spread a virus that kills off the majority of the human population and mate with the most beautiful women to create half-alien/half-human beings to replace those who have died.

Music researchers from a prestigious university develop an advanced artificially-intelligent program that can define hidden commonalities within music. After running the program for a few weeks, the A.I. discovers an unexpected result: more than half of the music in existence has distinct patterns which indicate that only one composer wrote it. However, for this to be true, the composer would have to be over a thousand years old. The research team is disappointed by this implausible result; but, after digging deeper into the findings and running a few diagnostic programs, you believe that the theory is, in fact, correct. Despite your colleagues' disapproval, you set off to find anyone who can shed light on this mystery, hoping that someone in the music industry can help you uncover the truth.

One morning, you woke up with your left hand gone. There was no blood or stitches. It was like your left hand had never been there in the first place. You look out the window and see a dog carrying your left hand in his mouth.

He looks at you and quickly dashes down the road. You throw on some clothes and start chasing him. The dog takes a sudden turn and goes into a wooded area. You continue to pursue, jumping over logs and dodging trees. You then come to a clearing in the woods with hundreds of left hands piled up next to a brook. The dog turns around, drops your hand on the grass, and stares at you in a funny way. You approach the dog and pick up your hand. Suddenly, all of the other left hands start to crawl around like spiders and begin chasing you. You run deeper into the forest.

A billionaire mogul loses much of his wealth in a legal battle with your family. To your mutual surprise, what begins as hatred turns into romance as you find a way to give him back the fortune he lost.

A well-respected scientist who discovered time travel decides to return to the past to meet his grandfather, a man who left behind an extraordinary legacy in academic circles. As he introduces himself, his grandfather begs him to stay in the past timeline and to help him with his work – academic work that brought the family much wealth and prestige. In the process, the scientist shockingly discovers that his grandfather conducts inhumane and immoral trials on people for the sake of acquiring knowledge. He wants to stop his grandfather, but he knows that anything he does may affect the timeline, including his own existence.

Your father is a famous scientist who invented a time machine. You ask him to take you back to when dinosaurs lived, and he does. You sneak one of the baby dinosaurs home with you in your backpack and hope your father doesn't notice.

When an alien humanoid species is discovered in a nearby solar system, you hear all about it in detail because your father was part of the team that discovered them. Now, some are being brought to Earth willingly, in an attempt to establish a collaborative relationship. You have been chosen as a liaison to help the adolescent alien feel more comfortable during his first days on Earth, but he doesn't seem interested in getting to know you. In fact – he seems outright strange and rude.

Your best friend is a physicist, and over the past few years he has become obsessed with a realm he calls the 'Otherworld'. One night over dinner, he attempts to convince you that he has found a portal into this realm and that he plans to go and explore this alternative reality soon. Worried about his mental health after this conversation, you begin calling him, only to get his voicemail. After he has not returned your calls for over a week, you decide to go to his house and check on him. He's gone, but he has left a note behind: 'I found the portal.' He also provides directions for someone – such as you – to access the realm and come after him if he does not return.

You work in an office with a coworker who annoys you with his political views that you disagree with. You complete a profile on a dating site and it pairs you with him. At first, you laugh at this, but realize that you are attracted to him despite his political leanings. You end up going on a date and having a lot more in common than you suspected you would.

Genetically-modified laborers built to withstand inhospitable work environments are already treated like second-class citizens, so it's not hard for people to find a reason to blame them for everything. When a serial killer strikes in the city, a quiet, modest mutant laborer who is well-liked in his community is named as the killer and is arrested. However, a high school student knows that this allegation is not true because she witnessed the crime. Now, she must prove the mutant's innocence while finding the true killer. Finding the real killer should be easy enough, though, since he's hot on her trail to shut her up, for good.

You are a successful career woman who's become a bit jaded, returning to your old hometown to try to find something you have lost along the way. You run into a high school crush who is now an unmarried pastor, and the reunion allows you to reconnect as you find that some things never change. This rekindled romance allows you to get your old self back, finding that faith and love were what you were missing all along.

You are part of a team of explorers commissioned to search for life-containing planets in distant solar systems. After traveling for light-years, your ship comes across a planet showing signs of life based on your preliminary readings. You are sent to the planet to investigate, but as you breathe in the air, you begin hallucinating mirages of past civilizations there that are now only ruins.

You are a dog walker with little interest in anyone with fewer than four feet. Your new client, the handsome owner of a goofy, flatulent French bulldog, changes all of that when you begin to bond over your loveable new charge.

A difficult home life has led you to make choices that have given you a bad reputation in your small town. Embracing this image, you have grown into a reckless troublemaker with a stony heart. At the town's annual fair, you hear an angelic voice singing a hymn that gives you goosebumps. You follow the voice and discover it belongs to the preacher's daughter, who you know is devoted to her faith. You are the last man she'd be interested in, but you can't ignore the attraction you feel to her. As you pursue her, she challenges you at every turn. Over time, your stony heart softens as the light of her love and faith fill your life.

A handsome widower moves into town and becomes active in the church as a channel for his grief. You become friends and try to help him heal and learn to love again. Friendship quickly turns into romance; however, the widower's faith and commitment are questioned when the father of his late wife visits and learns of the budding romance. His father-in-law believes that starting a new relationship is disrespectful to his deceased daughter. You must bridge the gap between these two grief-stricken men and prove that the new love you have established is not a betrayal of the late daughter's memory.

Your brick-and-mortar toy store is on the brink of closing down due to competition from big box stores and e-commerce. You know that this Christmas will make or break your business, so you are willing to try anything this season to keep things afloat. When the owner of the candy shop down the road proposes a partnership, you jump at the opportunity. He has been wildly successful over the last few years, and now he is willing to let you in on a few of his business secrets while promoting your toy store to his pint-sized patrons. One day, when you catch him glancing at you for a little longer than expected, you feel there is more to this partnership than just business.

Peering into the microscope, you find what appears to be a cluster of buildings within a dome-like structure. Shocked at this discovery, you decide to increase the magnification. As you focus the lens, you are astonished to see a man looking back at you with a large telescope, waving hello.

As you gulp down your second cup of ale, chaos breaks out in the village tavern. Someone you never thought you'd see again – a beautiful but ill-tempered warrior maiden with whom you fell madly in love many years ago – starts a bar fight. She and her two companions – a young squire and an enormous man with a missing ear – take on six local men over an unknown dispute. You don't want to help her, but she was your first love, and your protective instinct fires up. You jump in and knock out one brute after the next. Soon, you, the warrior maiden, and her companions are the last ones standing. She then notices you and tells you that she came to find you, but she got into a little trouble along the way. You're not surprised when she reveals that she owes the guys on the floor a little coin over a misunderstanding. You tell her it's been good to see her, but now you need to head home to tend to your father, who is worse off than the last time she saw him. She feels for you and tells you that is precisely why she's there. Your father lost his memory years ago in battle. Together, you and the maiden once sought out a bracelet that would restore his memory, but you both grew weary of your failures and fought often. You eventually returned home, and she returned to her clan. But now she's here, saying she's found the bracelet's location and wants you to come with her. Filled with renewed hope, you agree.

    There is a single, united galactic empire that spans and dominates known space. However, the ruler of this empire doesn't require the aid of regional governors, armies, or even police to enforce his policies. For reasons unknown to most, the emperor can create duplicates of himself at will at any point and time throughout the galaxy. Some days, he is just a few thousand people. Other days, he has a few million duplicates. All of these individuals act as one and effectively control billions of life-forms across multiple systems. However, the empire is threatened to the core when one of these emperors somehow gains independent thought from the rest and creates multiple copies of himself to overthrow the original emperor and to conquer the galaxy.

The murder of a regional governor who was en route to the capital planet has caused an uproar throughout the galactic empire. As the newest detective in the royal police department, you are surprised when the chief assigns this high-profile case to you. You have a sneaking suspicion that your inexperience is the reason why the higher-ups want you to be in charge of the investigation; they probably hope that the case will go nowhere. However, as you follow the leads and navigate the seedy underbelly of the capital planet, you realize that this is not just a murder, but an assassination, and that the emperor himself might be the culprit.

After the Siege of Paris, a Viking ship gets thrown off course by a large storm. The captain and crew are forced to land on an uncharted island. As they explore and look for food, crew members slowly go missing. As you look for the missing crew members in the middle of the forest, you find what seems to be an invisible wall. You decide to climb over it.

To improve your family's station in life, your father has arranged a marriage for you with a wealthy older man, but you don't want any part of it. You want to see the world! When a handsome airship pilot passes through town, he offers you the chance of a lifetime – fly with him and see the world.

The old lady who lives next door is always very nice to you, but she seems a little odd. One night, you look out of your window and see a rocket ship land in her backyard. Could your neighbor be an alien?

When you were assigned to the Galactic Peacekeeping Force straight out of the Academy, you thought you were in for a disappointment. At best, you thought it might be something like the American Red Cross from a century ago. You were wrong. Keeping the peace, it turns out, takes an incongruous amount of violence. Midnight assassinations, hostage rescues, escorting political targets, etc. But never something like this. The aliens arrive without warning, claiming that they need water. They choose you and your brethren – the Peacekeepers – to serve as intermediaries while they negotiate terms. Everything hangs on your team. You're assigned to security for the aliens; but, as you go to make contact with the alien emissaries, a band of alien dissidents warps in, plasma blasts your ship, and kills your commander. The aliens manage to put down the rebels – who are advocates for conquest – but you are left on a gutted vessel with tensions rising on all sides.

As governor of the most prosperous mining planet in the galaxy, your father is an admired and intelligent man. Everyone respects and listens to him, but for some reason you can't, even when you know he's actually right. Despite the vast luck of your birth and a lifetime of training, you want to turn your back on politics and become an explorer. Your father always says that true exploration is a hellish experience. The people who chart courses for planets have no idea what they'll find. They go to die so that others may live. You know he's right. The causes of death are endless, and it is probably your youthful inexperience that keeps you fixated on this idea. Still, you feel an inexorable flicker of excitement when the handsome chef's assistant tells you that he's joining an exploration crew. He's leaving tomorrow, and he wants you to join him.

Children's stories told of a time when the rain fell from the sky on its own. According to the stories, the planet somehow knew it needed water and sent rain to make the trees and plants grow. Adults laugh at the stories now and pay rainmakers like you to water their crops. However, more frequently of late, headlines tell of wildfires plaguing the west, just like they had before the rainmakers stepped forward to save the people they once thought of as invaders. As the largest fire in history advances on your ancestral native lands, you step forward. Yet you immediately realize that this is no ordinary fire. It breathes with the heart of the blackest souls, the ancient enemy of your people, and is looking for the strongest warrior. The rain dancers have not done battle since before the gold rush, but this land belongs to you, and you won't let the fires consume what's left of your heritage. You just might need a little help.

An alien who has been living undercover on Earth is able to maintain his human form for a limited amount of time each day before it reverts back into his original nonhumanoid form. He hurries home each day before this happens; but today, he's stuck on the commuter train that has broken down and there's no way off.

Due to overpopulation, civilization has collapsed and food has become scarce. Some people are resorting to cannibalism, while others turn to scavenging to survive. You are part of a group of scavengers and must teach others how it's done, while avoiding the cannibals hunting you.

You have lived for so long that it is hard to remember your childhood. Your first vivid memory involved being chased out of a village by an angry mob who thought that you were an immortal demon. Then, there was the time another angry mob burned down your castle because they thought you were a vampire. You've learned through trial-and-error that you must move out of a location and change your identity every twenty years or so. If you stay any longer, the locals begin to whisper about your never-aging appearance and come up with outlandish theories. One day, you are considering moving to a new town when you look outside of your window to find a group of people protesting. They think that you are an android, which were all banned and destroyed by the government fifty years ago. When the police arrive and start knocking down your door, you realize that your twenty-year policy might need to be adjusted downward.

You live in a colony that only allows one child per married couple. Your unmarried sister discovers she's pregnant, and the baby's father is already married with a child. Conceiving a child out of wedlock – as well as adultery – are crimes punishable by death for everyone involved. Now, you must take on the colony's government in order to keep your sister, her unborn child, and its father safe, even at your own peril.

When you dreamed of becoming a television writer, you never expected you'd end up wasting your time writing for a vapid dating quiz show – but a job's a job. One night, your very charming, very single boss asks why you're working late; you mumble something about new truth-or-dare questions. "Great," he replies with a smile. "Ask me one."

In a hidden government lab deep within the woods, a few human test subjects escape and roam the countryside. Disfigured beyond recognition, with no memory of who they once were, these man-made monsters begin to prey on the local townsfolk, tearing them apart limb by limb. As an on-duty police officer, your dispatch tells you to go to a nearby house due to a report of someone covered in blood being chased down by something indescribable. When you arrive on the scene, you open fire on the assailant and save the victim. However, after closer inspection of the deceased perpetrator, you find a tattoo of your name on her mangled arm. This was your wife, who inexplicably disappeared over two months ago. You vow to hunt down whoever did this to her and to exact revenge.

Stories abound about a dark planet that appears at random places throughout the galaxy and then disappears without a trace. No one seems certain what to call it. The Void. The Black. The Rivening. Hell. Hades. The Devil's Heart. But one thing that all the stories have in common is that no one who goes there ever leaves. Over the centuries, spaceships have launched probes into it, sending back footage of monstrous dragon-like creatures that would destroy anything in their path, but within a few hours the probes cease to function. You find yourself in the dead of space, with no engine and a restless crew. You've been sending out distress calls for two weeks when a planet appears before you, black and void. Life support can last only one more week, and it seems hopeless to wait for help, so you decide to land your ship on the dark planet.

Everyone knows about Akua, the immortal human being, much like how everyone knows about the King of England or the Pope in Vatican City. Maybe, in the beginning, people had questions, but now everyone has grown beyond the generations of questioning into a period of blatant acceptance. Still, you never thought you would get to meet her in your lifetime, let alone become friends with her.

You are a member of the most powerful monarchy in the world: the Danish royal family, who have ruled for centuries with dragons by their side. On your eighteenth birthday, you finally learn the family secret. Instead of being gifted a dragon, you turn into one.

You've been having vivid dreams recently about a beautiful girl. This morning in class, your teacher announces the arrival of a new transfer student. It's the girl from your dreams. She drops a folded piece of paper on your desk as she walks past you to her seat.

An immortal man, now hundreds of years old, has been living in secret for centuries, changing locations and names, and sometimes even faking his own death every once in a while. His main interest in life is drinking coffee, and he has spent most of his eternal existence traveling the world's coffee shops and cafés. When a global environmental crisis threatens coffee production, he finds himself forced out of hiding in order to save the one thing he loves.

You are a fighter pilot who is the subject of an underground experiment in which a bioship is created for you to fly. When you are flying it, the ship adapts to your movements like your own body would. However, once in space, the bioship turns against you.

Even as a smuggler, one thing you've never accepted is an escaped felon. One day in port, however, while the crew is unloading and you are lounging on the bridge, the door blows open and a woman stumbles in, bleeding from a wound to the gut and dragging a possibly broken ankle. Although she is dying, she is distinctly beautiful. She's also holding a pistol. Hurriedly – weakly – she orders you to take off. Your protests are cut short as she fires. A dart impales itself in your arm, but you feel nothing. She tells you that it's Alaya venom, which is famous for its slow but certain death. The woman says the antidote exists only on her home planet and that you have to fly there. All thoughts of negotiation vanish as she pulls another pistol – a real one this time – and assures you the next shot will not be so merciful. Seeing the madness in her eyes and hearing desperation in her voice, you realize she is a heartbeat away from killing you. Hurriedly you act, even though it means you will be left to fly the aircraft alone. The police give chase, of course. Now you are onboard alone with a strange, violent, and gorgeous criminal, headed toward a strange planet, with all the resources of the Empire aimed at bringing you down.

As a student of oceanography, you jump at the chance to accompany a crew on a deep-sea dive. Something goes awry on the journey down, however, and your submarine plummets miles into the ocean depths. On the bottom of the ocean floor, an onboard explosion forces you and the crew out of the submarine and into a small submersible. Another vessel appears to come to your rescue, and you realize there's a whole other world in this deep underwater, full of creatures you never even imagined existed.

Instead of the British Industrial Revolution, a magical revolution takes place in the late 1700s that results in the United States never becoming a superpower. Britain engages in a policy of isolationism, keeping all magical technology locked within its borders, while maintaining a dominant position on the world stage. As a British magic dealer, an opportunity presents itself in 1834, so you start illegally transporting bottles of elixirs into the United States and turning a huge profit – until something unexpected happens.

During the Victorian era, a man has been falsely accused of murdering his neighbor. His wife, desperate to prove his innocence, conducts her own investigation into the crime. Venturing into the castle ruins where the murder took place, she finds both clues and assistance from the long-dead residents of the castle.

On a self-sustaining ship, multiple generations have lived without ever setting foot on the ground, due to radiation from nuclear war. Earth is almost a legend, with some believing it was nothing more than a fairy tale. However, scouts have returned claiming that Earth is habitable again. The few remaining crew members from older generations are excited to return, while you and the rest of the younger generation are convinced that it's a bad plan and history will eventually repeat itself.

Nuclear war has irradiated the planet, leaving precious little land that is safe to farm or graze animals. You are part of a surviving colony that is located in the last uncontaminated and fertile region, defending your territory from those who would kill for it.

You are aboard a spaceship tasked with discovering new, habitable planets for humans. Your ship discovers an unknown planet which seems to be comprised mostly of water. After testing the atmosphere and determining it to be safe, you're sent with a group of divers to explore. However, you are entirely unaware of the creatures you will find beneath the water's surface.

On a cross-country road trip, you make one wrong turn, and then an entire series of wrong turns. Eventually, you stumble upon what seems to be a remote countryside, somewhere. The people there, however, appear to live in the Middle Ages and think you're a witch because of the

SUV you pulled up in. They won't let you leave, but you must find a way out before they burn you at the stake.

In an effort to counteract the effects of global warming, scientists release an aerosolized compound that creates a solar shield in the Earth's atmosphere. Unfortunately, they make a miscalculation and the sky is darkened, turning Earth into a frozen wasteland as all life-forms slowly die. You are one of the last climatologists and you attempt to find a way to reverse the blackening of the skies before it is too late.

Recent advances in medical treatments can reverse the effects of aging, essentially resulting in immortality for those who can afford it. As a result, the wealthy are finally taking a sincere interest in climate change, species extinctions, and other problems exacerbated by an expanding global population. Since the mortals greatly outnumber the wealthy and powerful immortals, the immortals are plotting to reduce the population of mortals, while the mortals are trying to gain access to immortality.

In the year 2146, androids have become commonplace on Earth. They are doing everything – from dishes and cooking, to flying aircraft and performing surgeries. The latest is a team of androids so sophisticated that they are said to 'learn' a person – to codify their identity into an algorithm and to befriend them. They are supposedly the most advanced machines to have existed, the first true relational A.I. Things go terribly wrong when you – a beta tester – and your family eagerly unbox and activate one. For the first four weeks everything goes splendidly; but, as the android 'learns' you, it attempts to alter your behavior toward what it deems to be more appropriate. It begins to subtly – and then not so subtly – reward good behavior, scold you when you fail, and eventually control you physically, though never with true harm or malice. Before long, you realize it sees you as its child. By the time you are locked in your bedroom with your family and promised a freshly-baked cake if you don't struggle, you must decide how to outsmart the super-intelligent mommy machine and power down the entire batch before the rest are activated.

You and your crew have just woken up from a ninety-year cryosleep. You've completed humanity's first intergalactic journey and are scheduled to return to Earth today. When you make it to the bridge, however, you realize the ship's A.I. system seems subdued. When pressured, it reveals that NASA stopped sending transmissions forty years earlier. It can find no signals from Earth. As you view the planet, you find it completely dark, with no signs of life. Alarm turns to horror as you land. People are everywhere, but they are frozen, completely unresponsive. This seems to have happened unexpectedly, leaving the planet a perfect tableau of what had been happening in that specific moment. Furthermore, monstrous creatures now roam the Earth and devour anything in their path. With only a dozen men, you must scramble to solve the mystery, and what you find convinces you that this was no accident.

You are a P.I. who's been hired by a wealthy family to find their missing son, a talented but somewhat reckless pilot and adventurer. His last-known location was somewhere near Tibet. They're paying you more money than you've made in the last three years combined, so turning them down is not an option. And, once you stumble upon the region where the son was reported missing, you become more determined than ever to find him, because the place is full of potentially dangerous prehistoric animals.

After a terrible storm, your fishing boat has run aground close to an island. You look at your navigation equipment, but there are no readings. You look at your phone's GPS and find the same result. You decide to swim to shore and search for help. However, when you finally reach the island, you are surprised to find no evidence of people, not even washed-up trash. As you explore the island looking for any signs of civilization, you have a persistent feeling that someone is watching you. You suddenly stop walking and listen. You hear a crunch as if someone has stepped on a twig. You quickly look behind you, to find a man in a three-piece suit staring at you.

"Good evening, and welcome to our resort."

"Resort? What resort?" you ask.

He then begins to twitch. "I'm sorry, but I must be experiencing a system error. What I meant to say was all intruders must be eliminated. Please stand by while I find something that will kill you. Do you see any good blunt objects I can use?"

You turn around and run.

Your friend has tickets to stay overnight in an old house that promises chills and thrills. She asks if you're game, and, of course, you say you are. Part of the stay includes a scavenger hunt that promises a cash prize if all of the items are found. As you move through the house, you discover a key that opens a sealed room deep inside. When you walk through the door, you immediately realize you're in a completely different time period – on a completely different planet – in a completely different reality.

A great flood occurs on Earth, during which most habitable land is submerged. Humans survive on vessels and in cities designed to float. From beneath the depths of the waters, creatures begin to emerge that are feared, but some believe that they are the old gods who are returning to help humanity and punish those who have failed to prove themselves to be worthy. One such creature attacks your floating colony, but allows you to survive.

Yes, you used to be in love with a vampire, but you were just seventeen and emotions were running high. You broke it off with him before you left for college and, although it was weird to go back to the real world, you knew it was the right thing to do. But then students at your college begin to go missing. Bodies are found on campus drained of blood. When your roommate and then your new boyfriend disappear, you've had enough. It's time to put on some garlic, grab a stake, and end this relationship once and for all. You just hope you can resist his irresistible charms.

In a future that offers mind transfer between humans, the government has decided to transfer adult criminal minds into orphaned children in order to be 'reeducated' on civil ways to conduct themselves. This decision goes horribly wrong, as children begin to commit heinous crimes – and you're tasked with ending the horror.

You are a lower-level lab technician in your pharmaceutical company, but you have always felt a sense of pride. They are developing something big here, and you are playing a part. For years, they were extracting chameleon DNA, splicing it into that of other animals. Eventually, they moved from reptiles to mammals. After failing for years to grow embryos in the lab, they've finally produced their first success: an ape born to two genetically enhanced parents that has developed the ability to change its color far more quickly and precisely than a chameleon. Corporate is pushing for human testing, but the majority of scientists caution against this course of action. Things go wrong when a geneticist is bitten by the ape. After a week in ICU, he seems to be doing fine, but then he begins displaying color changes. With each passing day, he becomes more erratic, suspicious, and ill-tempered. When he is asked to take a weeklong vacation to recover, he snaps and attacks the head of the department, biting his throat. From there, the condition spreads like wildfire, initially giving people superhuman senses combined with an ability to remain practically invisible, before driving them mad and giving them a bloodthirst only human deaths can sate.

Your family is part of a group of people who will be sent to create a colony on the moon. You're excited to go to a new place and experience such an amazing opportunity, but you're also nervous about all of the changes.

You are a rich merchant in medieval England and hire a servant girl to work in your shop. You fall for her and plan to propose to her, but rumors are she is a practicing witch. You don't believe it until you discover strange objects such as melted wax and bird feathers under your bed.

Stasis was created to keep the mind active during the voyage to Alpha Centauri, but when you woke, the memories of stasis were so vivid that your only desire was to return. The love of your life was a figment of that machine.

A deep space exploration vessel is thrown off course and ends up discovering a planet the likes of which has never been seen before. A city covers the entire surface of the planet, powered primarily by the planet's core, but there are no life readings. Excited to see this technological marvel up close and to find out what happened to its inhabitants, you and your crew decide to land on the planet and investigate further. When you open the hatch, the abandoned cityscape you were expecting is nowhere to be found. It was simply a projection of some sort emanating from a single structure in the distance. When you decide to launch and go back into orbit, your ship powers down. There is something draining the energy from your ship, and you soon realize that you and your crew have fallen into a trap.

It's been a long journey from the small town where you were raised to the big city where your burgeoning PR business is making a name for itself. But there's one complication you never could have planned for: the boy who shows up claiming to be your son. When his mother rushes in after him, you realize that, although you might leave your home, it never really leaves you. The preacher's daughter is as beautiful as she was at nineteen. You turned your back on her and her faith when you left the town ten years ago. But now, as you get to know the son you never knew you had and re-meet the woman you'd tried to forget, you realize that sometimes God's plans for you are a little more complicated than you'd ever guess.

The whale-like creatures that live in the temperate waters of your home planet have been hunted by aliens for generations. No one knows exactly why the aliens prize these creatures. All you know is that no one has ever stopped the hunt. Now nearly extinct, these last few remaining creatures have gathered off the coast of your hometown. Despite the aliens' advanced technology and your parents' refusal to help, you and your school friends vow to protect them at any cost.

You are a single parent with eight children. Eight. And he's the first person to take an interest in years. You have to deal with two grown children who think he's a creep, younger children who don't want him to replace your late partner, and your own reluctance to invest in a new relationship.

There is now a pill you can take that will trigger a genetic mutation to make you stronger, more attractive, and taller (over time). Your body is not responding correctly, however, and the growing won't stop. You're becoming a beautiful giant, but must try to find a way to reverse the mutation.

Studying animal species that don't experience the effects of aging has led to treatments to prevent aging in humans: by improving DNA repair, protein folding, immunity to cancer, and selectively eliminating old cells. As a result, human lifespans have increased by hundreds of years and the frailties of old age have been eliminated.

In an alternative universe, witches, wizards, and magic are the norm. Students study various magical courses at school. One witch, fascinated with magical doorways, rips a hole in the fabric of the universe, connecting this magical world to ours. The witch soon realizes that her non-magical double exists in our world, and she views modern technology as our own version of magic.

You desperately want to win first prize at the science fair, so you decide to break into your father's military lab at night using his password and keycard to look for ideas. When you open the lab's door, you find a cage with a strange blob-like creature inside. As you take a closer look, the creature wakes up and says, "Hi there! I'm Bob the Blob. Want to play with me?"

You smirk a little bit and say, "Sorry, Bob. I don't play with strange blobs." You begin to walk away, but you soon hear the cage door opening behind you. You turn around to see Bob out of his cage.

"Come on," he says, looking at you with a big goofy smile. "How about just one game of Parcheesi?"

The attic; under the bed; a closed closet. These pocket dimensions are invisible to most. You aren't most.

When your ship experiences turbulence during an ordinary military transport, you dismiss it as plasma imbalance, which is common between stars. Yet when you arrive on Earth, you realize something is amiss. It seems you actually passed through a wormhole into another time – a time when Earth hadn't yet begun to settle other planets. They've developed interstellar travel and are beginning to send exploration teams, but your home planet Turbiron hasn't been discovered yet. You are greeted as a hero and between you, your data logs, and your advanced ship, the people of this time are excited to learn about the future and enhance their space endeavors. However, knowing that the timeline is fragile and that any change in the past can greatly affect the future, you decide to launch your ship and escape Earth, preserving your version of history. Unfortunately, Earth forces disagree with your assessment and pursue your ship through the cosmos.

You hate his materialistic ways, but a billionaire's charm wins you over when, following an airplane crash, you are stranded for weeks on his family's private island.

It's a bright day. The village market bustles with merchants and traders selling all sorts of wares – fleeces, horses, cattle, corn, meats, and pies. You are on your way to fetch a sack of rare spice by order of your ill-tempered master, when two masked men ambush you and steal the schillings your master gave you. Never one to back down from a fight, you chase the hooded figures throughout the market and eventually end up in a dark alley. When cornered, they reveal themselves to be members of the Oath Guard – a sword-wielding secret society from the other side of the world. They tell you that your father was their leader before he was slain by your master using dark magic, who then kidnapped you while you were an infant and made you into one of his many slaves. It took more than a decade for the Oath Guard to track you and your master down, but now that you have been found, it is time to exact revenge. "You were able to chase us down in the marketplace, so you do have raw potential, kid. The question is, do you want to help us?" Without hesitation, you say yes.

You and your neighbor have been at odds for years over the state of his front yard. You can't stand how it looks and are convinced that he is a complete slob. Meanwhile, the neighbor believes that one of your kids is tearing up his yard. One day, in the middle of yet another argument, you both witness a gnome come out from behind a bush, rip up a piece of the lawn, shake his fist at both of you, and run away. After a little investigating, you learn that a small colony of grumpy gnomes is responsible for all of the damage, but no matter who you talk to or how much evidence you provide, no one believes your story. When you find your house covered in dirt one day, you decide enough is enough. Reluctantly, you and your neighbor put your differences aside and decide to track down the gnomes before they wreck your entire neighborhood.

You wake up in a stasis pod, your memory swimmy and scattered. You remember who you are, but vaguely. Nothing fits or makes sense. You are interrupted by Commander Tranton, who marches into the corridor and barks everyone into order. Apparently, there was a problem with the stasis pods, and, while he was able to save your lives, certain neural pathways may have been distorted or altered in the unfreezing. There is, however, a mission at hand. You are part of a decades-old rebellion. Yours is one of the sole surviving ships to strike at a key Federation mining planet. As the mission progresses, you get a strange feeling. The Federation soldiers seem terribly desperate, and your own crew is vast and well-equipped. After capturing and questioning a few enemies, you realize something is not right. Breaking away from your squad and sneaking back onto the ship, you realize the stasis pods didn't malfunction; they were designed to erase your memory and replace it with a fabrication. You start to wonder who is fighting for what and who you really are.

You are forced to make a decision when a group of your fellows returns to the ship, hunting you down.

While exploring space to find other life-forms, your vessel is hit by an undefined force and goes wildly off course into unknown space. After you regain control and assess the damage, you learn that the ship's engines are unable to achieve light speed and you cannot contact the rest of the fleet. After several months of traveling below the speed of light, your crew runs out of resources and the ship's power containment begins to degrade. With no other viable options, you and your surviving crew members board escape pods and land on an uncharted planet, hoping to find help from the local inhabitants.

While herding sheep, you find an old dagger. When you pick it up, it becomes warm in your hand, and you feel a swirling deep within your body. Your father races into the field to knock the dagger from your grasp. You become confused when he scolds you for touching it and refuses to listen to your protests. Hurt by his lack of trust in you, you go to bed without dinner, only to slip into a fitful sleep filled with ominous shadows with glowing yellow eyes, flying witches, and creatures cackling in the underbrush. The screams from the nightmare slow to a gurgle as you wake to the stench of wet fur and decaying meat. You jerk upright when the door shatters, revealing a chittering crazed animal-like monster. It storms inside, its claws searching for your flesh. You react without thinking, moving your arms with seeming practiced control. You parry and block the monster's attack until your hand delivers a final blow, burying the dagger deep in the monster's chest. You step back, staring in shock at the bloody dagger still in your hand, wondering how it found its way to you. As its power fills your body, making you feel invincible, you realize it is not important how you got the dagger, only that it is here with you, now and forever. Gurgling screaming interrupts your thoughts, and you rush into the front room, where your father is on the floor, blood covering his chest. He coughs up more blood as he tells you to follow the pull of the dagger. Your tears fall as he takes his last breath. The dagger tingles in your hand, signaling that your journey is just beginning.

Before the Earth was made uninhabitable, a group of survivors evacuated the planet on a spaceship. Generations later, it's finally time to send a team down to test for habitability; but upon landing you discover that there were survivors who never left.

Your writing career has been stagnant since you moved to the city, so when your editor comes to you with a project unlike any other, you hope this will be your big break. The assignment? An exposé on a bachelor billionaire tycoon that everyone in the city is talking about. The goal is to uncover something unseemly about his background and ruin his reputation. You feel bad about it, but if this is the price for success, you decide that you are willing to pay it. Besides, the public deserves the truth, right? But when you pose as a high-end real estate agent and manage to get some time with him, you find that he's smart, charming, and considerate. He's nothing like you expected. The more time you spend with him, the more your feelings grow, until you realize you're unable to complete your assignment. But if he ever found out about your true background, your budding relationship would be doomed.

There's been a rash of break-ins at your store. The police officer they keep sending is gorgeous, funny, and kind. Everything you're looking for, but how do you make the first move? You keep tripping the alarms! Great plan, until you find out it's totally illegal, and you're about to be arrested by the handsome cop.

The galactic empire was once the shining beacon of the universe. Now, after years of over-expansion, war, and infighting, the government is on the brink of collapse. In order to keep its citizens in line and to prevent mass rebellion, a strict code of conduct has been instituted which prohibits all activities that are not specially sanctioned by the government. Protests occur across the capital world, but, as head of the military, it is your job to shut down the activities of these activists and to maintain the fragile order. You know that the people would support you if you decided to overthrow the government, but your honor and loyalty prohibit you from doing so. When you hear that your allies within political circles are backing a revolution, you know that it is your duty to report this to the emperor, despite the fact that it will mean their execution. There is an important choice to be made, but you are unwilling to make it.

A romantic flight in a young pilot's plane turns harrowing when he and his partner get trapped in a storm. After a controlled crash-landing, the plane is out of commission, but the lovers find themselves in a remote mountainous area. According to their GPS, they are in a Kansas farm field. However, that is far from the case. And, when they encounter the local inhabitants – both humanoid and otherwise – they know that they are "not in Kansas any more".

We discover that beneath its seemingly uninhabitable appearance, Mars has an entire race of subterranean alien life-forms living in it. You are part of the team sent to explore this civilization.

You should have known it was too good to be true when the caretaker dropped the price of rent in half, but after your disastrous relationship fallout, you need a fresh start, and the tiny village of Adare in Ireland sounds perfect. The village is straight out of a fairy tale, and you quickly fall in love with the spirit of the people and the land. As you explore the village and its hidden treasures, you stumble across castle ruins that hum with life. In the basement, you find a cheval mirror covered in dust. It has odd-looking Celtic runes on the sides. You know a few of the runes and speak them aloud. As you do, the mirror begins to ripple like water, and you are transported through time. You are immediately captured as a spy and taken to the king, who is as ruthless as he is handsome. You have to convince him to spare your life so you can try to make it back home, but at what price? And with the heat that flares between you and the king, you may have to decide where home may truly be.

With heavy firepower, your crew has landed on a planet known to have hostile aliens that seem reptilian in their appearance. The terrain is comprised of swampland and the reptilian beings live underwater. You've put on a protective wetsuit and you're now leaving the ship to explore for the first time.

While you are attending an elegant soirée at an old mansion, a servant runs out of the kitchen screaming that the house is on fire. You turn to run, but you can't find a way through all the people and smoke. Just as part of a wall is about to fall on you, a handsome stranger saves your life, sacrificing his own in the process. Afterwards, the stranger appears to you in your dreams and begs you to come back to what is left of the mansion.

You just scored a spot on a major competition TV show that makes its participants do the craziest things. You're partnered up with a handsome but over-confident stranger who, you decide, you instantly despise. Can you work together to win the day and the huge prize?

Biohackers have stolen DNA samples from the world's most prominent leaders in order to clone them and eventually replace them on the world stage. As the Physician to the President, you stumble onto this conspiracy after performing a DNA analysis of the President and finding trace elements of this cloning procedure. You then contact other doctors of world leaders and ask them to run the same test. Most of the physicians encounter similar results, except for the Prime Minister of Great Britain. You know that this may be the last opportunity to identify the biohackers, so you fly over to London and set a trap before the last prominent world leader is replaced.

You are scheduled to host a Steampunk panel discussion at a comic book convention, when you notice something odd about the back door to the meeting room. You struggle to open the door, and suddenly you and your fellow panelists are pulled into a vortex that sends you to an alternate, Victorian-era reality.

Your father helped reveal a traitor during the last Succession War, and your family was rewarded with a position governing the Empire's most recently discovered planet, a remote place abundant in resources and beauty. When you arrive, you find that the settlement is under constant attack. Farm burnings and night raids threaten this once idyllic place. Some say that the cause is rebels from the Succession War; others say it is aliens. You are convinced it is just an ordinary band of criminals, but when you and a few new school friends begin to investigate these crimes, you uncover a secret darker and deeper than you could have imagined. As you follow the clues in a desperate gamble for peace, you begin to wonder if the Succession War itself might have been a lie.

A quiet stranger moves to town and joins your grief group. As a widow, you're open about your struggles and how the church has been there for you. The new man never says anything, but attends every meeting and every Sunday service. Despite his stoicism, you find yourself drawn to him. God works in mysterious ways, you've learned, and there's nothing quite as mysterious as the stranger in your parish.

In the near future, mind transfer is possible, but only from human brain to machine. There are some levels of consciousness that do not transfer, such as empathy and love. The resulting A.I. is not quite human at all – but something far worse – and the appeal of immortality is causing too many people to undergo the process. You work in the laboratory where the transfers occur and, with the help of a few close friends, decide to sabotage the system.

With the world moving toward a more perfect civilization, parents of childhood athletes are facing a moral dilemma. Sports science long ago developed optimal methods for training, rest, and recovery in each sport, so the major differentiating factor is genetics. Ambitious parents are carefully selecting the genetic characteristics of their children before birth to maximize success in a selected sport. But as these athletes grow older, their genetically engineered competitive nature has led to vicious attacks on and off the field.

News breaks across the world that a team of scientists has created a portal to an Earth-like planet in another universe. Interestingly, this planet is a carbon copy of Earth in terms of its history and its population, with only a few differences here and there between the two planets. When a delegation is sent from this parallel world to Earth and is interviewed on TV, you are surprised to find out that one of them looks and acts exactly like your late husband. You quickly pack your bags and travel to the portal, hoping to reconnect with your long-lost love.

From your fiancée's perspective, you are a baron – a man born into power and influence. But nothing could be further from the truth. Five years ago, you were hunting for venison when a horse suddenly came out of nowhere and galloped past you. Curious as to its origin, you followed the horse's trail back to an overturned carriage with bodies strewn across the ground. The scene spoke of a horrific massacre. You open the carriage door to find an entire family of nobles slaughtered. Whatever the robbers wanted, they left no witnesses to tell their tale. However, one particular young man bore a striking resemblance to you. Then it dawned on you: if you could pretend to be him as the sole survivor, you would inherit these lands and become a nobleman for the rest of your days. You took a hard look at the corpse, making sure that your face and his were a perfect match. It was like looking at a reflection. You worked to change clothes and dispose of the corpse, then waited to be rescued, finally being found by a group of knights, who brought you back to the city and your castle. You have ruled there ever since. Those who knew your doppelganger could not tell the difference. Any inquiries into your past resulted in you claiming amnesia brought on from the carriage robbery assault. And now, you are to be wed to the finest maiden in all of the kingdom. This maiden, however, is not what she appears to be. She was once the leader of a gang of criminals – the same criminals who robbed and slaughtered your adopted noble family. Now she has come back disguised as a duchess to kill the remaining witness of her crime and finish the job once and for all.

Your grandfather died when you were twenty-five and left you with an old pocket watch. When you opened the watch for the first time, you thought that it was broken because the hands quickly spun counterclockwise. When you closed the watch and looked at your phone, you noticed that it was twenty-four hours in the past. You attempted to try it again, but the pocket watch would not open. Years later, a tragic accident claims the lives of your family. You tell yourself you can undo this, as you try to open the pocket watch. It opens; however, this time the hands quickly spin clockwise.

It's the year 2521 and time travel has finally been perfected. Laws preventing changes in the timeline have been passed and the time police guard it carefully. A young girl time travels to the future and becomes good friends with her own great-great-granddaughter. The time police are in hot pursuit as she attempts to escape them, not realizing that her own descendants' and new friend's existences are at stake if she is arrested and sent to prison.

You are the fifth wife of King Henry VIII, but no one knows that you are actually a powerful sorceress who has been all the king's wives in different forms and will do anything to influence the royal family.

While out walking one night, you come across a comic book store that you've never seen before. You enter, and the odd man behind the counter offers you a free, limited-edition Deeds and Dwarves Campaign book, the game that you and your friends play every weekend. You take it, envisioning yourself as the champion of your friend group who will be applauded for showing them exclusive content for a game they all love. After planning a campaign, you gather your friends in your mother's basement, which is home to your family's four cats and their respective kitty litter boxes. But the moment you finish filling out the character sheet, the room begins to rumble, and suddenly your mother's basement is plonked down in the middle of Dwarfguard, the fictional land of the game. Even worse, your friends are transformed into their dwarven characters, the cats are transformed into horses, and you have become an old wizard with arthritis. None of you will be turned back until you beat the campaign, so you slowly climb onto your meowing horse and set forth into a world of adventure.

A biotechnologist creates a program that can be downloaded to a device and inserted into the human body to induce repair of genetic mutations. The results are so effective that the biotechnologist's life is threatened by those in the medical industry who are losing money as a result. You vow to help him in exchange for a copy of his program to fix your own genetic disorder.

Your life didn't work out the way you had planned. Instead of being a successful race car driver, you are now flipping burgers at a fast food joint while your social life and love life are non-existent. Your only form of enjoyment comes from playing video games – and you are grateful for the escape. When the first virtual simulation game hits the market, you are excited for a whole new level of distraction. This simulated reality game requires you to perform tasks physically in real life to unlock achievements in the game, and you feel pain when injured. Your skills that normally go unused in real life make you a top player within the gaming world, and you draw the attention of a fellow female player who you fall for. But will your relationship be able to translate into the real world, or are you doomed to experience life through a simulated reality forever?

After several decades of genetic research and experiments, humanity was able to develop superheroes with powers that no one else thought possible – everything from telepathy to super-strength to super-speed to telekinesis. Basically, everything you could find in a comic book. At first, these superheroes protected the innocent and stopped crime. However, over time, the superheroes became belligerent, fighting amongst themselves as well as against the people that they swore to protect. Eventually, they overthrew governments, took control of countries, and turned into warlords who invaded one another's lands. As a high-ranking general of one of these war-torn countries, you are forced to commit atrocities on behalf of your 'superhero' leader, who has the ability to manipulate time. Then you realize that this situation can all be corrected by placing a standard mind control device on your leader's head, which will allow you to ask him to do anything, including sending you to the past to stop this timeline from ever happening. It is a long shot, but you and your fellow soldiers are ready to try.

After many years and several trials, you invent a device that is capable of taking photographs of an alternative universe. This universe actually exists within our own universe; however, there is an interdimensional barrier that prevents one from bleeding into the other. The universe you witness through your photography can be described only as catastrophic: a bleak, jagged wasteland filled with nightmarish creatures and dark skies. There is no color to speak of, and you find nothing that seems natural in this world's harsh nature. One day, you notice that there is a man in the background of one of your photographs. You zoom in to find that he is holding up a sign that reads: 'You are collapsing the barrier. Stop!' The man is missing from the next photograph, but you can see a deer and a green patch of grass where he once stood.

The Black Death creeps deeper into the English countryside each day. The men in the village build a barricade across the road to keep travelers out, but you know that won't stop what's coming. It's not a disease – well, not in the traditional sense. Someone sent this plague south, and the northern warlocks are following behind, wiping out any resistance as they roll through the country to take it all as their own. What they really want, though, is The Book, which is your family legacy. You'd be burned at the stake if your fellow villagers knew you had it. However, you knew this day would come. You open The Book and recite the spells as you prepare to do battle in secret, hoping to save a village that would kill you for what you are.

You've purchased an old house that's on the historic registry and needs a lot of work. As you uncover its years of use and abuse, you find messages on the walls that appear and disappear, even though you're the only one living there. You ask a nearby handyman for help in deciphering the mystery, and romance ensues.

Obsessed over a girlfriend who dumped him on prom night, a mad scientist discovers a way to recreate his love interest from the body parts of others. Through the use of nanotechnology, the scientist reanimates dead tissue and adheres it to a robotic skeletal structure which is controlled by an A.I. that matches the personality of his old flame. Now all he needs are the right body parts. After finding a woman with a feature that resembles his old crush, the scientist murders the woman, severs the body part from the victim, and places it in cold storage. After a few years, the scientist has gathered most of what he needs. All that is left are her eyes. Unfortunately for you, your eyes bear a striking resemblance.

The goblin infestation that has plagued New York City for more than a century has nearly come to an end. Most would say that is a good thing. The disgusting creatures spread disease, hang around in alleys, and tip over dumpsters to feed their insatiable appetites. They were a pestilence to be eradicated – at least that is what the government has been preaching within their public service announcements over the years. However, nothing could be further from the truth. Although their exterior is unpleasant to look at, they are as human as you or me. Yes, they harbor disease – because it is illegal to give them medical care. Yes, they live in alleys – because no one would allow them shelter. Yes, they tipped over dumpsters – because they were starving. You have decided to give the goblins shelter, hiding as many as you can in your basement. You could go to prison for harboring the 'unclean', but these goblins have become your family and your only true friends in an insane world.

Your teachers began to worry about you in kindergarten, when you were unable to move your building blocks with your mind. By the time you turned eight, you were diagnosed with a rare syndrome that prevented you from wielding magic due to the absence of a magical aura. But that makes you unique. In a world where magic is the means to almost every end – from warfare to simple household chores – your lack of magical ability means no one can sense your aura or feel you coming. You can slip past any magical barrier, completely unnoticed. Your strength and agility greatly outmatch those of most individuals, whose dependence on magic has left them physically weak. In other words, you are the perfect spy.

You have been having sleepwalking episodes ever since you moved into an old fixer-upper, and you constantly wake up exhausted. You install a camera and try to see what you do while you are asleep. You are surprised to discover you have been going out of your bedroom and having a relationship with a mystery man that appears to live in your house. Who is he?

Your friend can't wait to introduce you to her new beau. She's been talking about him nonstop and you're actually a little nervous to meet him. When he walks through the door, your jaw drops. You would know that face anywhere.

You are a single mother who works as a waitress at a nightclub to make ends meet. The one thing you can't stand are people who get everything handed to them, like the rich, snooty patrons you have to wait on night after night. However, when a handsome and charming club-goer becomes smitten with you, you find yourself drawn to his enigmatic way. After a few coffee dates, you wonder if this could be the one, but then you learn that he's actually the club's billionaire party boy owner – a man you've heard about and hated from afar for years. He swears he's changed and that he has fallen for you, but you're not convinced. Can you trust him to leave his partying lifestyle behind to become a family man?

Unfortunately, your father is about to croak. As the leader of your clan of frogs, he reveals a shocking secret to you on his deathbed: all the males in your family can turn into a human – but only if they can convince a human to fall in love with them.

You are a young girl on a student scholarship at a very high-profile British university. One day at the uni pub you meet a handsome young man with whom you feel in love at first sight. Next day, you open the newspaper, only to discover you have been out with a crown prince.

You and your best friend have a sleepover in your backyard treehouse. She brings something cool to show you – a huge leather-bound book of supposed spells you can say, some of which can transport you to a different time in history or a different plane of existence altogether. You personally think it's a bunch of baloney, but in the spirit of a spooky Friday night sleepover, you're game to try some of the spells out. You find one that promises to transport you to a land of perfect peace and harmony. You just need to gather a few items first. After everything is ready, you chant the words, and, to your shock, you find yourself standing in what looks like a busy, futuristic city. You don't see one single human being, but you do see plenty of robots.

The new guy you have been dating has invited you to his house for a home-cooked Italian meal. You put on your cutest outfit and head over in anticipation of some cannoli and canoodling. He invites you in and offers you a drink, and then his mother walks out of the kitchen with a tray of antipasti and a scowl.

You prefer the dark loneliness of space to your crowded home planet of Earth, so you've agreed to be a scout for an organization looking for resources to mine on other planets. On one such scouting trip, you discover a planet with much potential. However, when you land, a ghostly fog surrounds you, with voices calling you deeper into it.

You always thought of death as just a vast nothingness, a rest that was eternal. When you actually die, however, you find that this isn't the case at all. You wake up – exhausted – and realize that you're still on Earth. You're incorporeal, and no one can see or hear you. You are a ghost. You get over the shock quickly enough, and then boredom sets in. In fact, you're absolutely out of your mind with boredom. Years and then decades pass as you roam the streets. One day, many years after you first awoke to this pitiful excuse of an afterlife, someone looks at you – not through you, but at you. Then he speaks. He can see you. You're determined to know why. As you get to know him, for the first time in ages you feel love.

As part of a fleet of explorers, you encounter an alien species that is far more advanced than humans. They have found ways to heal all diseases and do not participate in war, leaving the beings to survive far longer than the human lifespan. Believing they have much to teach you, you wish to stay on their planet, causing conflict within your fleet.

Your dance group rents out the church basement for practice every week, but you've rarely ventured above into the church itself. Religion has always made you uncomfortable, and you generally avoid it at all costs unless it is part of a wedding or a funeral. However, a scheduling mishap, followed by a desperate pastor looking for volunteers, leads you to help out with the church bake sale. While organizing the event, you meet a handsome parishioner who challenges your lack of faith and opens your heart to greater possibilities.

For two long years you searched deep within the Fagaras Mountains for what many thought was just legend: a simple door standing alone in the middle of a clearing. Before you embarked on your search, you were a blacksmith with a loving wife and three children. You had become a prominent and respected member of your village, but nothing was never enough. You always wanted more than what you were due, so one day you decided to throw your stable life away. You abandoned your wife, your children, and everything else you once held dear, to search for the door. But when your supplies were running short, you returned to town in the dead of night and stole whatever you could get your hands on. When one of your former neighbors cornered you, you killed him in cold blood and ran back to the mountains. However, all of it was worth it now that you have found the door. According to the legend, if you open the door and enter, you will be granted what you truly deserve. Knowing deep down that you deserve it all, you open the door.

You are the ultimate killing machine, a cyborg created for one purpose only: to eliminate the enemy. Your next assignment is to kill a billionaire financier who has dabbled a little too much in politics. You arm your plasma rifle and storm his mansion. To your surprise, he is not there, but you do encounter a small child in her playroom. "Would you like to play tea party with me?"

Tea party? Tea party does not compute, so you turn around to walk away. But you realize that you could use a break. Plus, your target is not home. So you put down your rifle, your knives, your grenades, and your laser sword, and play tea party with the child. You love it, so you play more games with her. When her dad comes home, you resist your programming to murder him outright and instead hide in the playroom's closet so you can play more fun games with your new best friend tomorrow.

A colony ship is pulled out of hyperspace and encounters a monstrous creature: a large mass of tentacles that spread out from what seems to be an unblinking eye. For weeks, there is a standoff as repairs are made to the ship's engines. During this time, a few colonists on board the ship communicate with the creature through prayer and seances and believe that it once lived on Earth and was known as the Kraken. As the Commander of the ship, you are skeptical of these reports, until the creature begins communicating telepathically with you. You are suddenly compelled to steer the ship into the mass and be consumed by it, but you resist the creature's mind control.

You've never given faith much thought. You're not exactly atheist, but you wouldn't claim to be agnostic either. You're just uninterested. But when an accident leaves you hospitalized until you're able to heal, you meet a nurse who cares for you, holds your hand gently, and prays over you. You wonder if there's more to this universe – and yourself – than you ever knew. If there is, you think she must be the key.

You've worked years to get to where you are as hairstylist to the stars. It's good work that pays well and lets you help your family back home with their financial struggles. Plus, you love the work. The only downside is that the patrons of your salon aren't exactly easy to talk to. Their priorities are so different! Vanity plagues their every move, and their cavalier attitudes drive you crazy. No one is worse than your weekly customer: a billionaire obsessed with his aging appearance. He's handsome and you know from overhearing a dozen phone calls that he's pretty charming, so you can't quite understand why he's so insecure over a few wrinkles. You tell him as much, and he's surprised to learn that you find him attractive. He asks you out and, despite the age difference, you find yourself saying yes. Over time, you help him find the confidence he needs. You discover that you share much in common, and love grows.

The Council of Mages gathers on the top floor of its massive Manhattan skyscraper every ten years to conjure a list of all the families in New York City, ranking them according to magical ability. The list includes many sections, with subsets and sub-subsets of magic-wielders, but only the top and bottom truly matter. Families at the top are granted wealth and station and are invited to work directly with the Council to shape the future of humanity. Meanwhile, families in the bottom five percent are deemed a hindrance to societal evolution and are taken away, never to be seen or heard from again. Your family is only mildly magical and has always been somewhere in the middle of the list, which is fine from your perspective. Despite being the strongest mage in your family, you've never had more aspiration than working a nine-to-five job. But when the new list is announced and your girlfriend's family is pushed to the bottom five percent, you know you have little time before they come to take her and her family away. The Council sees all. Defying them is unthinkable. The only chance is to leave the city. Most die trying to cross the bridges into New Jersey, but you have no other choice. You won't let them take her.

Scientists have figured out how to transfer an aging mind – with all of its memories and mental abilities – into an infant clone. While these patients get a healthy new brain, they must start over with an infant's body and physical abilities. After multiple mind transfers over hundreds of years, some mind transfer patients decide to give up their physical bodies and enter the afterlife. A new industry has been built around erasing the brains of these mental elders, and selling their young adult bodies to the highest bidder.

You're in charge of organizing this year's Rockefeller Center Christmas Tree lighting. When one of the singers scheduled to perform during the show flakes out at the last minute, you scramble to find a replacement. As you work through your rolodex, finding that – not surprisingly – every singer you know is unavailable, you worry that the lighting will be a disaster. Then you find one person who says he can be there in fifteen minutes and pull off an *a cappella* performance – but only if you go on a date with him. With no other options available, you agree.

You sip your coffee at your favorite hole-in-the-wall café across from a crumbling and congested elevated highway. It's nearly midnight, but you don't want to go home. Your heart is aching. Your grandmother has been taken by a man your kind knows by reputation but no one has seen up close – a fallen angel who will hunt down anyone or anything if the price is right. The owner of the café, an old woman with a weathered face, offers you another cup and a smile of sympathy. When a scruffy-jawed man with thick boots and violet eyes enters the café, the old woman nearly drops her coffee pot. The café owner calls him by name, the shock in her eyes palpable as she begins to tremble. The man nods a greeting to her. Then he notices you and, to your surprise, marches right over to your table with an aggressive, animalistic intent. You hop to your feet and quickly whisper an incantation. He stops in his tracks and smiles, as much as his gruff exterior will allow. "I haven't picked a fight with a Benandanti in a hundred years. Why would I start now?" You slowly sit back down as the man makes himself comfortable in the opposite seat. "Word on the street is that you are looking for a man with broken wings. I have a lead or two, but first, could you help me with a little something?" He takes off his fedora to reveal two horns sprouting from his head. You wave your hands, and in an instant the horns disappear. "Thanks, buddy. Now, let's get to work."

There is not much known about the alien spaceship housed in Hangar Bay 2. It crashed on Earth about thirty years ago. No one knows how to turn it on. There is no propulsion system or fuel. There are no doors or cockpit, so it must have been piloted by some sort of A.I. The eggheads at the Pentagon think that it was not built for war, but just because it does not have lasers and bombs does not mean that it does not pose a threat. From your point of view, a robot spaceship crashing on your world is a provocation in and of itself. This is not the best way to say 'Hello'. However, everything you think you knew about that spaceship changes when a new report comes across your desk from a hotshot scientist. She claims that she has found a way to interface with it and that there is an internal clock counting down to zero. What happens at zero is anybody's guess, but all we know for now is that the countdown will end next week.

It's the height of the witching hour, risky for an ambush, but it's your job as a witch-hunter to take risks. Suddenly, you're frozen by magic. You see a familiar face, only to hear, "I'm sorry. I do love you." The world goes black.

The galaxy was abuzz when NASA first announced it had finally cracked the secret to creating a wormhole, but no one's tried it yet. However, once created, the wormhole will remain open, allowing humanity to pass through it any time they wish. NASA claims they can control where it opens. They say it will serve as a bridge to the adjoining galaxy, allowing human expansion to make an unprecedented leap forward. Unfortunately, opening a wormhole requires an immense gravitational force, the amount that can shatter planets and send ships careening out of control. Nothing as large as a black hole, but something far larger than Earth. A very large sun, for example. And there's the catch: someone needs to fly toward the heart of a sun, open the wormhole when they reach critical momentum, and pass through it without knowing what's on the other side. You've been chosen to take on this mission.

The Huns race over China. In a last vain attempt to save the outermost borders, the emperor calls for the armies to assemble. Everyone knows you to be a clothier, but your family has a history older than recorded time. Your great-grandfather used his magical gifts to counsel emperors, as his ancestors did before him. Your family has never ruled, but their influence could be seen in the very heart of China's history – that is, until the emperor's daughter accused your great-grandfather of dealing in all things 'unnatural'. In fact, such an accusation was the farthest from the truth. Your family's gifts come from the heart of China, the very soul of the country. As the Huns press further into your country's borders, you know that China is calling for you to fulfill the oath of your ancestors. You may have to stand alone and defeat the invaders without help, but you will face the Huns. China gives you no other choice.

He ran his hand through your hair, commenting on its softness, and from that moment you were hooked. You had no idea he owned a vast empire of real estate and was looking to find the perfect lady to settle down with.

Scientists have mastered the art of repairing or replacing all human organs except for the brain. Over a typical lifespan of two hundred and twenty to two hundred and eighty years, the brain acquires damage that eventually leads to dementia. Luckily, human cloning is simple and inexpensive, so it's possible to transfer your aging mind into an infant clone. You retain all of your memories and mental abilities, but start over with an infant's body and physical abilities.

Aboard your stranded spaceship, you begin to notice metal turning into a biological substance resembling trees and vines. An invisible alien entity that has made its way onboard is helping you create a sustainable biological atmosphere to keep you alive until you reach a habitable planet.

You and a group of spacefaring humans discover a planet in the far reaches of a neighboring galaxy. On this planet, you find an elven civilization that has lived in relative peace. You are introduced to the elf queen, who informs you that her forefathers used magic to flee Earth from your kind thousands of years ago. You get to know her and her civilization over the course of a year, but when it is time to leave, the queen begs you to stay. She fears that if you go back home and tell your people about what you have found, the elves will be threatened again and forced to abandon their world. You assure her that this will not be the case, but when you find that your spaceship has been sabotaged, you realize that it might be more difficult to leave than you had originally thought.

Genetic modification of animals has produced monstrous results, leaving the world's human population hunted by gigantic, predatory beasts. Since humanity now must hide in fear, technological advancement has declined and humans have returned to nomadic tribes in order to survive. You live in one of these tribes, but have discovered an abandoned, dying infant beast alone in the woods. You attempt to revive it and eventually bond.

The colony you live in has decreed that its current population exceeds the planet's available resources. As a result, the government begins systematically exterminating the elderly, the infirm, and the mentally deficient. You work on the government's death squad and discover a loved one's name on your list.

You are an artist living in the thirteenth century who has been summoned by Llywelyn the Last, the newly anointed Prince of Wales. When you arrive at his castle, you find a group of eight other draftsmen, some of whom you know by reputation. Llywelyn explains that there have been sightings of strange creatures across the land, and he wishes for them to be documented for further study. You are not experienced in drawing wildlife and would rather return to your work on the Lambeth Apocalypse manuscript, but you have no choice but to obey the commands of your liege and join the expedition. You are sent on horseback to the last known sighting, accompanied by some of the royal guards. What you find is stranger than you could ever have imagined. Multiple-legged animals with humanesque faces. Wings on creatures never meant to fly. Some draftsmen are so sickened by the vision that they abandon the expedition altogether, believing it to be the work of Satan. The remaining party investigates further and eventually uncovers a group of sorcerers merging animals and people together in ungodly ways. No one knows for what purpose, but you are determined to find out.

Nanotechnology has provided the military with unprecedented capabilities, including suits of armor that grow from bands around the arms and contact lenses that give thermal vision, night vision, map overlays, and team chats. But one thing it can't do is replace your leg. You've been a Federation sniper for as long as you can remember, but when you lost your lower left leg to an old landmine, your contract was discreetly terminated. For your own safety and to protect their secrets, the Feds wiped you from their records. That's why, when the coup happens, at first the rebels miss you and a few other premature discharges. When you are discovered and they realize that you know government secrets, you are forced to leave your family in hiding and bring together the survivors. With this motley band, you are stretched to your limits, relying on what nanotechnology you can scavenge to defend yourselves and lay a false trail.

Deep in the core of the Earth, ancient beings have aided humanity throughout its existence and have helped us to discover fire, fusion, antibiotics, and many other scientific advances. These beings are shapeshifters – sometimes they take on the form of lava, sometimes they take on the form of rocks, and, most often, they are invisible to the human eye except through our dreams. As you drill down to the center of the Earth, you hope that you encounter one of these beings and beg for its assistance in ridding the planet of an evil wizard who has taken control of the surface world.

As a demonic angel-hunter, you do not know the difference between right and wrong. You have been raised and trained from birth to kill those in the white robes, but then one captures you before you can kill him. He makes it his mission to change you, and over time your demonic features recede. Hate and rage are replaced by kindness and understanding. Your dark red scaly skin becomes human-like in appearance. When your horns fall off, your angel captor decides to release you. Yet you refuse to go, as your love for him has blossomed during your transformation. You know that other angel-hunters will pursue him once they learn what has become of you, and you are determined to defend yourself and your love from these demonic forces.

You are the youngest and only female of six siblings. You and your five brothers are the children of a beloved tavern owner who is an exiled knight. He taught each of you to handle a sword with precision. Your blade never leaves your side; it's a part of your soul. One day, your eldest brother makes a foolish wager with an enchantress, who unleashes a curse upon your entire village, leaving all the men weak of mind, muscle, and spirit. Hearing of this, a gang on the outskirts of town decide to raid your village and take what they can. You attempt to gather the local women to fight back, but most refuse. The ensuing raid devastates your small village, leaving much of the town in flames. Before riding off, the gang chieftain demands a monthly tribute; otherwise, they will pillage the village's food supply and poison the wells. Lost, you go to your sanctuary by the lake and pray for guidance. There, you find an alchemist who gives you a small stone, which glows a brilliant purple before transforming into a magnificent sword. The alchemist tells you that the women will listen now, as you were born to be their leader. Fire burns within you. You and the group of women you assemble will not go down without a fight!

You are an alien and the 'new kid' in school. You are very nervous because you don't look like anyone else, and you can't understand the language of your classmates. Some kids in your class invite you to play ball with them at recess, and soon you find that you aren't so different after all.

There was an old lady who lived in a shoe – until its owner returned. After a long hibernation, the giant came down from the mountain to find his forgotten left boot inhabited with pests. Enraged, he gave the old woman and her many children three days to vacate the shoe. Panicked, the mother didn't know what to do. However, her children hatched a plot. They attacked the giant when he returned in three days and demanded that he let them keep their beloved – albeit stinky – home.

During a business conference in the Greek islands, you hear a sweet and soft song floating on the air from a distance. You walk down the beach, following the sound, and find a woman in the water beckoning you to come closer. You move closer, before sitting down on the beach to listen to her voice. Days pass and you become too weak to stand. Nevertheless, you remain entranced by this creature. Suddenly, her singing shifts to crying, and she tells you that, although she is the last of her kind, she cannot bear to devour another victim. You vow to help her, not knowing if the love you have for her is true or is a result of the siren's curse.

A vast galactic empire that spans the known reaches of the galaxy has fallen into the wrong hands, ruled over by a tyrant who has been granted unlimited power through his discovery of an alien artifact. You are a thief and a rebel intent on stealing this instrument of power from him to end his tyrannical rule.

Soldiers are now trained in virtual reality-simulated environments for maximum experience and efficiency. It's terrifying, but perfectly safe – until a virus is planted in the software, and the soldiers become trapped inside the simulated environments. Safety goes out the window when the simulated threats become real and start attacking them.

Human augmentation is all the rage, with people replacing human body parts with cybernetic alternatives. As an ambitious entrepreneur with significant financial backing, you have come up with a business idea that is sure to make you millions of dollars: body part recycling. You have built a large processing plant that can break down human body tissue into a slurry, which can then be used in a wide variety of applications: from fertilizer to cattle feed to even plastic alternatives. Surgeons from across the world have signed on and are now sending over discarded arms, legs, and other body parts to your facility. Business is booming and you are planning to launch a much-anticipated IPO soon. However, when workers from your processing plant hear strange noises emanating from Vat #4682, you think that the chemical additive that you just started using may have unforeseen side effects.

On vacation, a family spends a couple of nights at an old Irish castle which has been converted into a hotel. While exploring the castle and the grounds, two siblings discover a secret passage and a stairwell leading to nowhere. When they decide to explore again that night, they see a portal open at the top of the stairs. They decide to enter this portal, and they are then transported into an alternative world where the castle exists within a magical kingdom. There they meet two strangely familiar children their own ages.

By law, robots and humans are strictly forbidden from falling in love with each other. That's what you've been taught your entire life. A hundred years ago, humans could marry robots that were custom-built to be the perfect companion. However, after the birth rate plummeted, governments across the world banned inter-intelligence (or artificial and non-artificial) relationships. However, when technology reaches a point where you can no longer tell the difference between man and bot, you end up falling for a robot. You will do anything to be with your one true love, despite the risk. Will you be able to keep your love a secret, or will you pay a high price?

You've had foreign language students before, but none as handsome as the son of a billionaire inheriting all of his father's wealth. When he asks you to be a translator for a trip he's about to take, you're all in.

A chance encounter brings you onto the radar of a tortured young billionaire who can't forget the abusive past he endured at the hands of his father. You have a similar past – can you move past it together?

Your elders have raised you to hunt vampires, who are the closest thing to a demon that you will ever encounter in this world. According to your elders, vampires have no morality to speak of; all they want is to feed. You are hardwired to hate these evil creatures, until you meet one and learn the truth. They only drink the blood of those they want to mate with, marking their territory. When one of them drinks your blood, the passion instantly runs through your veins, and your life changes forever.

Earth has not yet reached the stage where an interstellar journey can be achieved in a single lifetime, not without the use of cryosleep. There's also no return journey yet, which is why they send mostly criminals and anyone else crazy enough to go. Yet you've always wanted to go, and when you graduate with a triple-doctorate in astrophysics, aeronautical engineering, and biology, you cannot help but feel you're wasted on Earth. You're stuck doing hypotheses, proofs, and theoretical formulas, while criminals are out there tasting and testing the real thing. You ask for a position leading the next expedition and are ecstatic when they accept. The problems start when you meet your crew and begin to understand just why these criminals are being sent away from Earth. They've displayed good behavior for five to twenty years in prison and now want to live just like you, but no two of them agree on the way to do it, and they're certainly not going to listen to you, with your spotless binder, neatly pinned tie, and fingers uncalloused from a single day's work.

You and your friend are in different relationships that are unhealthy. When you get together, you are constantly sharing stories about how miserable you are. Finally, it dawns on one of you that you should be with each other because you have much more in common with each other than with your partners.

Under the flicker of torchlight within your clan's cave, you paint the history of the great battle beneath this cycle's moon. It took twelve hunters to defeat the mighty mammoth. The first eleven hunters had been thrown and knocked out, as usual, leaving you, the final hunter, to pull power from the moon to finally bring down the beast. It was better that way. You don't want anyone to know what you can do. But then a curious child follows the hunters on the next hunt and sees the power of the moon fill you. Things become complicated, as you don't want to be revered as a god or feared by your clan. When a horde of a hundred outland warriors threatens to push your clan from their fertile hunting grounds a few days later, you and the moon may be the only thing that can save them – until the curious child steps beside you and starts to glow.

The assassin came at midday, shooting the Empress from three miles away with a drone that could have been controlled from anywhere in the solar system. You've never seen technology like this, and some of the higher-ups suspect it could be alien-created. Fortunately, the nanobots implanted in the Empress' body a couple of months before the assassination have the capability of recording the memories of the host. You have access to everything she saw, heard, felt, and lived for the last eight weeks. Now it is up to you, one of the Empire's top detectives, to relive the Empress' final two months over and over until you identify and catch those behind her death. You desperately wish you could do more than watch, but you can only sit there, an observer, as if watching through a dream.

Many years ago, a select few people were chosen to be part of a unique experiment. Each heralding from a different region of the world and of varied cultural and socio-economic backgrounds, the subjects were given what has now been confirmed to be the elixir of life. Originally thought to merely extend life, the seven subjects have instead become immortal after ingesting this potent elixir. With their friends and family dying decades ago and life becoming increasingly monotonous, not all of the test subjects are happy about the outcome.

A couple have been dating for about three years, and the man still hasn't proposed. The woman is getting impatient, and after a drunken night out on the town, she proposes to him. He loves her – but he says no, owing to his belief that it's a man's job to propose. This awkward moment leads the pair down a path neither expected.

Life is hard, especially for a single mother, but you've made the best of it and took a new job as the secretary for a billionaire. A terrible tragedy rocks his world and you're there as a shoulder to cry on as he heals (and falls in love with you).

The Great Food Crisis resulting from a world-wide drought left the world in ruins, causing millions to perish from starvation. Eventually, government and modern society collapsed, leaving scattered nomadic tribes throughout the world. As the son of a chieftain, you hope to one day unite all tribes and work together to bring peace and prosperity to what is left of humanity. However, your father tells you that uniting under one banner is a nearly impossible task. Frustrated by your father's point of view, you go for a walk along a nearby lake. In the distance, you see what can only be described as an enchantress wading in the water. As you approach, she hands you a sword and says, "Excalibur once helped unite humanity hundreds of years ago. Use it to unite humanity again."

Immortality treatments are now standard care for humans, just like childhood immunizations, dentist visits, and birth control. This has amplified disparities between the rich and the poor. The rich spend their lives indulging in hobbies that are well supported by their trust funds. Meanwhile, the lower- and middle-class struggle to make ends meet for an eternity. As a result, suicide rates are skyrocketing among the poor.

Things get odd one lazy Sunday afternoon when a team of government officials informs you they need to excavate your backyard, something to do with decades-overdue cleanup from the Settlement Wars. They want to ensure no salvageable equipment was left on anyone's land. You shrug and give in, returning to your family at the dinner table. The Feds have been at their work for four hours when there is a shout and a sudden explosion. Quickly, you run outside; but, reaching the porch, you stop in shock as eight forms resembling massive metallic eggs shoot up into the air, each buzzing and whirling madly, before coughing, spitting smoke, and falling to earth. There is a crackling, hissing sound, and tentacled, bug-eyed creatures emerge, catching the Feds in their tentacles and tearing them to pieces. You quickly urge your family into the basement, snatching your shotgun from the mantle and tossing the wood axe to your wife. Waiting to see if the creatures have noticed you, you realize you must somehow protect your family while warning the government there are still aliens hiding on your planet.

You are a private eye in the heart of the city who is often tasked with scoping out adulterers, people who skip out on their girlfriends, or shady business deals. When a young woman comes to you, teary-eyed, in the hopes of finding her missing boyfriend, you don't bat an eyelid, even when she says she can't pay your entire fee. The case is as typical as typical can get. But when she tells you how he went missing, how he quite literally vanished, screaming, into thin air, you accept her meager offer and get to work. You poke around, visiting his local haunts, and eventually witness something rather shocking: a man in an alleyway talking to tiny, fluttering forms who, when he doesn't comply, seem to zap him with something. He screams out in pain, vanishing into a cloud of mist. You watch a little longer and discover that the small creatures are fairies. Digging into the magical underbelly of the city, you find a retired warlock who says he can help you go undercover. You hesitantly agree. Once you are in your tiny, winged form, you have three days to find the group responsible for these disappearances.

Your grandfather, a legendary archaeologist in his day, recently passed, and you're going through his manor to organize his things according to his will. In the attic, you find the large floor-length mirror he mentioned in his last letters to you; he told you he trusted it with no one but you. You quickly find out why – it's a portal to the exact time and place where the mirror was made. You find yourself in a small European country in the middle of a war. You can't be sure, but you think it might be the late Middle Ages. You have to find an item he mentioned in his will before the portal closes, trapping you there forever.

You are mad at the world and he's an eternal optimist. While on a business trip, you get stranded in the same hotel room (thanks to a hurricane) and the ensuing hilarious encounters convince you to join him in romance (and optimism).

After a nuclear apocalypse, you are part of a group of survivors dealing with the after-effects of an irradiated planet. Many have grown sick from the radiation and died. There are some, however, who appear to be completely unaffected. You were a doctor before the war and are determined to use your knowledge to find out why.

Ever since you moved into your new apartment, you have received an anonymous letter each week that predicts future events. Some of the predictions are benign, such as 'You are going to have a great time at the movies.' Others are more helpful, such as 'Stay away from Chinese food this week unless you want to be sick.' You have enjoyed the letters and speculated about their origin. As you open the latest letter, you are surprised by its tone. There is only one sentence: 'Leave the city now and run for your life!'

All your life you've felt awkward and out of place. You are always the last one chosen in gym class, always sit alone in the cafeteria, always on the outside looking in. Then your adoptive mother enrolls you at a new school, where you meet two girls with the same birthmark that you have on their necks. You look nothing alike, but you know you are kin. You can just feel it. You decide to invite your new friends over for a sleepover the night of your sixteenth birthday, which happens to coincide with the next full moon. That night, after a few good scary movies and far too much pizza, you decide to camp out in the backyard beneath the moonlight. After everyone has fallen asleep, you are awakened by a haunting voice beckoning you, telling you that your reunion has restored your gifts of sight. Frightened, you wake up your new friends. Then you notice her standing there: your queen, the goddess Hecate. She smiles serenely at you before speaking. "Hello, my Fates. It's good to see you again. It's time for your first quest – in this lifetime."

After the great interplanetary war, a human colony on Mars gained independence from Earth and immediately severed all ties and relations with their home planet. A thousand years later, Earth receives a message from the lost colony, inviting a delegation to a summit. The government of Earth decides to send a small group of diplomats, including yourself, to this colony in the hopes of reuniting humanity.

The Earth's sun is dying and a mass exodus is underway. You're the pilot of a carrier ship charged with moving people to new homes in various colonies in the nearby galaxy. Your route requires you to travel through a dangerous space corridor infested with alien pirates determined to steal your ship and enslave your passengers. Can your excellent maneuvering skills, coupled with help from a spunky female mechanic, save the day?

Ever since you were a child, you've loved the big old house on the outskirts of town. You dreamed of living there and obsessed over every detail of the house. Your second-grade teacher was even concerned about your obsession, especially considering that every picture you drew in class was of that large house on the hill. As an adult, you come into some money, so when the house comes on the market, you quickly call up the seller and agree to buy it. It is what you always wanted, and now you can finally live there and slowly renovate it over time. The man selling the house recently inherited it from his deceased grandmother. When he gives you the keys, he tells you that the house has a funny effect on people, so he'll stop by to check on you later. You find him a little odd, but charming in a sort of endearing way. Yet that night you begin to understand what he meant when you hear a whisper coming from the hallway. You get out of bed and put your ear close to the bedroom door, but all you can make out is: "Welcome home. We missed you."

A nefarious corporation has discovered biomechanical technology that, when implanted, forces subjects to join a 'hive mind' and do what they are told without question. Your friend is one such subject. To save your friend, you need to find a way to pull him out of the hive mind, while avoiding detection by the people who are under its control.

Stalactites and stalagmites made of crystal-clear ice fill the tunnels of this underground civilization. Electricity seems to run on a mysterious, glowing plasma-like source. As the first outsider of your kind to journey this far, you strive for acceptance. Still, you fear you may never be able to return home to share all that you've learned.

According to legend, the world was created by three ancient dragons, each representing a different element of reality. The World Dragon carved the terrain with his claws, the Water Dragon flooded the craters her brother had created, and the Air Dragon created the winds. Life sprouted in the lands crafted by the dragons, and soon the world was teeming with creatures of every shape and size. However, the Water Dragon became furious with her younger brothers for letting life flourish within their domain. She hatched a plot against all who lived, including her brothers, to flood the world with poisonous water so that she could live in solitude. Her brothers heard of her plan and cast a spell that rendered all three of them dormant so that the beings who resided on the lands they had made could thrive. The world and life upon it continued unabated, and soon the settlements of mankind began to take root. Prophecy states that there will come a time when the Water Dragon will awaken from her slumber and attempt to flood the world once more. At that time, a champion of immense power will fight the Water Dragon and defeat her once and for all. But none have been born with any such ability to do so – that is, of course, until you come along. Your powers emerge when you reach adulthood, and when it is discovered that the Water Dragon's dormancy is coming to an end, you must fulfill the prophecy.

Working as a paranormal hunter is hard enough without throwing romance into the mix, but when a fairy you recently banished starts stalking you on the job, you realize something has gone wrong. In your overworked state, you messed up the pronunciation of a single word that turned your banishing spell into a binding contract of marriage in ancient fairy lore. To break the unwanted union, you and your new spouse must travel to the fairy world, where you encounter all the fairies you banished – who now want revenge.

As a mechanic living in one of the galactic empire's many slums, you are content with your ordinary life. You'll never do more than repair spaceships, but as long as you stay off the secret police's radar, you are in good shape. That is, until a young woman appears at your door one night and tells you that you are the rightful heir to the empire. You ask for evidence, and she shows you the results of a DNA analysis which prove that you should have inherited the empire. Your biological mother, who was the empress at the time, feared for your life and gave you away to a common family in order to protect you. You ask how she knows this information, and she responds that she is your cousin and that she stumbled upon all of this within the royal palace a year ago. Your cousin has a network of supporters planted throughout the government who are ready to overthrow the emperor and put you in his place. "All you have to do is to be onboard," she says. You quickly shut the door and lock it.

You are a busy bank clerk with no social life, but a great love of reading fiction. One day, you read a book about a fairy. As you keep reading, you find yourself gradually falling in love with her. One day, she flutters into your bank.

You travel to England and stay in a castle that's been converted into a B&B. You enjoy your time there and find the other guests downright charming, especially the man you bumped into at the airport who surprisingly was staying at the same B&B. One day at breakfast, one of the guests starts chatting about how he used to be a lamplighter in Bristol. "A lamplighter? You must be well over a hundred years old, or maybe electricity isn't in fashion in Bristol," you joke. All of the guests at the breakfast table suddenly stop what they are doing to stare at you.

Then, the lady who runs the B&B slowly approaches and whispers in your ear, "You are upsetting my patrons." You apologize and get up to leave, but she pushes you back down into your chair. "I'm sorry, love, but leaving is not an option." The room goes black. A person from the other side of the table lights a match. It is the handsome man from the airport. You ask what is going on, but he knows as much as you do. Together, you look for a way out.

A group of élite soldiers is sent on a reconnaissance mission to a remote location in the jungles of Africa to investigate the disappearance of several tourists. Though they're experienced in hostage rescue and recovery, they're completely unprepared for what they find: a village of robots that time traveled from a distant future. The robots release the hostages and explain that they are trying to hide from a tyrannical government which has decreed that all A.I. life-forms should be disassembled. The robots fear that some day their temporal coordinates will be discovered and that they will be fully eliminated. The soldiers vow to protect these robots at all cost.

The galaxy is filled with brave heroes, daring rogues, and sinister villains. Swashbuckling adventures occur almost every day, but you couldn't care less. You never wanted to follow in the footsteps of your father, who is an evil, all-powerful galactic emperor. You would rather just work on your garden or play badminton than vanquish your enemies. However, due to your father's expectations, you begrudgingly accept your fate of being a bad guy. You become famous for your dastardly deeds and soon earn a fearsome reputation, but the reality could not be further from the truth.

It is said that when the world eventually falls into darkness, there will be one who will come from the light to lead humanity out of it. You. You are the Prophecy, an angel who is the sole salvation for the human race. You have been under constant threat of destruction. Demons and dark forces hunt you endlessly. It is a battle just to survive. However, when a demon corners you and confides in you instead of attacking, you lower your weapon and listen. "You are wrong about all of this," the handsome demon states. "The Prophecy foretells that you will be the cause of humanity's downfall. All humans and demons will perish, and angels will rise in their place. What your brethren have told you has been a lie. Join me, and together we will make our own destiny together."

An advanced race of beings is demolishing planets to build pathways for warp-speed travel across its vast empire. Your home planet is next in line for destruction, so you take part in raising an army to protect your home.

While exploring space, a ship's crew members begin to develop extraordinary sensory abilities. Some are frightened and overwhelmed by this experience, while others welcome the feeling of seeing music vibrate in the air and hearing the frequencies of colors. You are a writer who is feeling these changes and attempting to capture the experience in your journal, but you find it hard to describe.

You are a public interest journalist writing about the same things over and over again. Lost dog found. Local team wins a championship. The guy next door wins the lottery. You yearn for more, something more captivating and interesting, and one day you finally get your wish when you are sent to interview the owner of a mysterious house that has become a local legend. The house never changes and has always looked brand new, just like the pictures from the 1700s before the town was built up around the original estate. The man who lives there looks strikingly like his father, his grandfather, and his great-grandfather before him, leading to tall tales about who he really is. A chill covers you as you are invited inside. Everything looks new except for the wall clock, which doesn't seem to tick. The man gives you a cup of tea, and you sit beside a window looking out over the back lawn, but there is no grass or gardens on this summer day, only snow. You set your tea down, gaping, as the man sits beside you and starts to explain.

Deep sea technology locates a strong magnetic force emanating from a fallen space rock in the ocean. When it is brought to the surface by divers for further investigation, the space rock begins to grow and take on a baby-like appearance and manner. The scientists name him and one even takes the baby home to raise him. When he begins school, his superhuman strength and clumsy demeanor bring about unintended consequences.

The DNA of hundreds of thousands of species – both living and extinct – has been fully sequenced and made publicly available on scientific databases. Computer analysis has identified DNA sequences that code for thousands of poisonous proteins, similar to ricin and botulinum. Dictators and terrorists are now producing large quantities of these biological poisons. You command a military unit responsible for tracking down and destroying these poison caches.

The apocalypse occurs while you're in a shopping mall, which then becomes buried beneath rubble, trapping everyone inside. As different groups form and fight for dominance, how long can you survive on Orange Julius and Sbarro?

The cause of the dinosaur mass extinction is a present-day scientific mystery. Some say it was an asteroid, while others speculate that it was a massive bout of volcanism. However, you know better: this happened because of you and your time machine. Now, primates have evolved into an advanced species instead of your dinosaur forefathers. With your species wiped off the face of present-day Earth, you vow to restore the timeline.

Alien life-forms have started making themselves known, although they've been in our midst for centuries. The way they've stayed hidden is they shapeshift into felines, and have been observing us undercover in their roles of house pets and street dwellers.

Farm 'animals' have undergone so much artificial selection that they are now essentially bags of meat that feed from food trays. These animals are cloned in labs, so their miniscule brains no longer need to interact with other animals or the natural environment. You have discovered a new virus that produces no symptoms in the cloned animals, but that leads to serious neural degeneration in humans after years of exposure. This virus is already present in farms across the world.

The new world your crew has discovered is full of angel-like beings who move gracefully and are fiercely protective of humans. They have visited your world multiple times in the past (thus inspiring stories of guardian angels) and this is the first time you're visiting theirs.

New technology has made it possible for our dearly beloved pets to remain alive as long as we do. Failing body parts are easily repaired using nanotechnology. One woman, wishing that her cat could talk, programs a group of advanced nanobots to augment her cat's speech capabilities and verbal comprehension. Her attempts work, and the sassy cat becomes a famous sensation that eventually gets a little too full of herself.

Fantastic creatures have gone extinct, but their DNA remains preserved in samples from museums, labs, dry climates, and permafrost. While the DNA is somewhat degraded, modern methods can accurately sequence degraded DNA, reconstruct it, and insert it into living cells – including oocytes that can be implanted into surrogate animal mothers. Let's welcome back saber-toothed tigers, woolly mammoths, dodo birds, and more.

You never learned to swim, but signed up for adult swimming lessons despite your misgivings. Your instructor is a drill sergeant-type who seems to think you're training for the Olympics, but the only other student helps lighten the mood. You begin to grow fond of the student.

Aliens have landed on Earth and they are all female forms. In an effort to return human tribes to matriarchal cultures, they enslave all the men and elevate women to positions of power within the government.

"Would you rather live a normal lifespan and die in your eighties, or relive the same month for eternity?" asks your best friend in one of many games of Would You Rather.

You never expected that when you responded, "The same month!" you would be binding yourself to a contract of a never-ending October. You relive this month over and over again, feeling cursed and hoping to somehow break the cycle.

The Lord of Hiccups is known as such due to the never-ending hiccups inflicted upon him at birth. Your sadistic uncle forces you into a marriage with the cursed lord and, after one long year, you have had enough of your husband's never-ending ailment. You go on a quest to find the only known cure for such a curse: the Holy Dixie Cup.

A reclusive billionaire without family or friends is in a wreck and develops temporary amnesia from the injuries. Without any identification, he falls in love with you, the nurse who nurses him back to health. As his memory slowly returns, he realizes that friendship and love have been missing from his life, and he has found both in you.

Witches and wizards, warlocks and dragons – they're not what you've seen in storybooks. They're real, but it's not magic. It's science – developed over thousands of years on the distant planet of Madoopalus. As Arthur C. Clarke once wrote: 'Any sufficiently advanced technology is indistinguishable from magic.' Born into an evil wizarding family hell bent on taking over the planet, you must betray your family to save the world.

Devout your whole life, you're dedicated to preaching and spreading the gospel. But when a new man moves to town with a dark and mysterious past – and no patience for the community you've built – you're faced with your toughest challenge yet: love and cherish a man who is against everything you stand for. With a burly exterior and matching attitude, he tries to fight against your efforts to draw him closer, until suddenly you both realize there's more at stake than just a religious conversion. To be together, there's always a give and take, but can you get through to the man you're developing feelings for? Or is love not on the cards?

As the newly coronated queen, you grow tired of the silly games women must play to keep heroes satisfied. You especially dread the annual hike to the dragon's lair, having to yell for help all day long until a hero shows up to 'save' you. Throughout the kingdom, women and make-believe villains want to put an end to this farce once and for all. Therefore, you enact the Princess Act, which declares that women are no longer required to carry out damsel-in-distress scenarios to boost the egos of heroes. Shocked to hear that women were pretending this entire time, heroes must now find a new way to prove themselves.

After years of tireless trial and error, you believe you'll never discover the secret to time travel and are ready to give up – until you go to bed one night and wake up in the year 1890. You finally did it, but you don't know exactly how. Maybe you left your prototype turned on overnight and it somehow worked remotely. Or, maybe, just maybe, someone from the future sent you to the past right before your eureka moment to prevent you from discovering time travel. You have many theories, but, for now, you're trapped in the past without any of your equipment. You must build a time machine made out of gilded-age technology and get back to the present.

On the night before graduation, you and your best friend try to conjure up a unicorn in the basement of the mage's school. You're thrilled when it works... then quickly panic when five unicorns appear, then ten, then twenty. Soon, the entire castle is overrun by unicorns doing everything from raiding the castle kitchen for apples to chewing on tapestries and knocking over priceless magical artifacts. Knowing that daylight is only a few hours away, you and your friend have to find a way to send these clumsy magical horses back to their world before the headmaster wakes up.

As a sexton living in Florence during the Renaissance, you have always been fascinated by art, especially the murals found at your workplace in the Brancacci Chapel. One day while working, you notice an extra figure in one of the murals. When you see the mural the next day, the figure has moved closer. You see it again in the evening and, to your surprise, the figure is even closer. The man looks like he is running for his life. Certain that the others would call you crazy, you keep quiet. But the next morning you see the torso of a man emerging from the wall, struggling to break free. He begs you for help, his body half stuck in the painting. When you pull him from the wall entirely, he dusts himself off and runs away. You are about to pursue him when you see something from the corner of your eye: a large group of people have suddenly appeared in the mural. You turn around and stare at the new figures. They seem to be chasing the man and are increasing in size ever so slowly.

When the U.S. finally cracked time travel, they contracted you – a retired Navy SEAL, one of the finest linguists on the planet, and an expert in navigation – to join their team. They're sending you and your team back ninety million years, to the age of the dinosaurs. Fear and excitement abound as you explore a land far more fascinating and bizarre than that of existing theories. Then a rocket comes roaring out of the sky and lands before you, revealing a truth that sends you into shock. Humans didn't come after the dinosaurs or even coexist with them. They bred them. Vast ships orbit the Earth, traveling to and from a distant planet – humanity's true home. Dinosaur meat is considered a delicacy, and Earth is one of the few planets suitable for breeding them. When you are caught up in a sudden battle, you realize these advanced pre-humans are at war – a war that will eventually destroy the dinosaurs and bring on the Ice Age.

You're a practicing atheist, which means you avoid all churches, spectacles, and other religious nonsense that rages on around you. But when a freak storm traps you and the pastor in a cabin with nothing but a fire and conversation, you realize that things might not be as they've always seemed. Maybe, just maybe, there's something to what the woman is saying. The light of day seems too bright, and a promise to attend worship with her brings doubt, but you've got to try. You realize that a connection this deep has to count for something.

A pandemic virus has struck humanity and the world as we know it has been entirely overrun by wild and escaped animals. Humans have been seriously weakened, but you are a survivor and must find a way to leave your shelter to find more resources before you starve.

Many decades ago, humanity sent a gigantic spacecraft with a population of over ten thousand people to colonize a recently discovered Earth-like planet in a nearby solar system. The journey was expected to take over three hundred years to complete. During this time period, the ship's advanced ecosystem would sustain the passengers across many generations. As the third captain of this ship, you tire of the seemingly endless journey through the void of space, and so you ask your lead scientists if there is any way to get to your destination faster. After several years of research and experimentation, the scientists report that they have found a way to increase engine efficiency, and you order your engineering team to immediately begin implementing this new design. You are excited about arriving at the Earth-like planet during your lifetime, but there are some crew members who would rather live and die within the confines of the ship than to settle a harsh, untamed world. From their perspective, abandoning a spaceship that provides everything that they need is reckless. Home is not some faraway planet. Home is this spacecraft, plain and simple. You will have to convince them otherwise before mutiny becomes an option.

In a post-apocalyptic future, food is scarce. Riots have made cities dangerous, and roving gangs have formed to take control of limited resources and territory. You and a group of other survivors have discovered a warehouse full of provisions and are determined to protect it at all costs.

A cyberattack has occurred in which anyone who focuses on a signal from their smartphone or television is immediately and irreparably hypnotized. You are part of the team sent to find the signal's source before more people die of starvation in their hypnotized state.

A music industry mogul hears your voice on a demo album that he receives and signs you to his label. Your troubled life and past keep him at bay for a while as his friends warn him against it, but true love can't be held back for long.

She's not sure exactly how she made it through cadet training, but a bookworm finds herself on a military starship sent to the far reaches of space. Her anxiety-ridden personality and socially awkward demeanor are in striking contrast with the rest of the ship's crew members, and she soon feels ostracized. A clumsy moment in the mess hall gets the captain's attention, and he orders you to take this new crew member under your wing and to build up her self-confidence. You are not very comfortable with this particular order, but you do see potential in her, despite her nerdy characteristics.

You've spent your entire adult life traveling through space to find a way to become immortal – and, surprisingly, you find it on a lesser-known planet on the other side of the galaxy. You travel back to Earth, excited to tell the world about what you have found. However, upon your return, you realize how much time has passed on Earth. All of your loved ones are gone, and you begin to question choosing immortality over the people you cherished.

As a senior detective in the special victims crimes unit, you are hunting down a serial killer who targets young college women. The clues lead you to a reclusive billionaire with a 'devil-may-care' attitude. But something is off. It's just too neat when all fingers point to him. However, you can't help but question your motives as you find yourself drawn to him in ways you've never felt before. Can you put aside your own desires to find out if he's really a serial killer, or will your passion get in the way of doing your job?

You've just moved into a fixer-upper in a quaint neighborhood. You're looking forward to the project of building and designing your nest. Everything's perfect… or would be, if it weren't for that gorgeous but obnoxious guy next door, who's also remodeling his house and who you fight with practically every day.

On the capital planet of a galactic empire, a glittering playground for the rich has been built to provide its wealthy inhabitants with a pampered lifestyle. However, this city has been constructed and maintained on the backs of slaves kidnapped from the empire's other planets. You live on one of these other planets, and when your brother is kidnapped by slavers, you will stop at nothing to rescue him.

In less than a week, society as we know it has fallen. Since all forms of electronic communication are down, there's no way to know exactly what has happened, but you heard explosions all over town and can only assume the worst. But your significant other is on the far side of town and it's time to brave the unknown to get to her.

After arriving on a distant planet, a colony of humans escaping a toxic Earth are welcomed and aided by an alien civilization. As the years go by, the human population explodes and their excessive use of resources overwhelms their alien benefactors.

After a lifetime of running from your family's traditional expectations, you find yourself in the one place you never thought you'd be: the sanctuary of a church. You've got nowhere else to go and no one to turn to – except, maybe, the one thing you've been avoiding. The handsome pastor promises to help you find your way again. You slowly realize that sometimes the road less traveled is the one you were always meant to go down. With the promise of love, faith, and happiness on the horizon, you have to ask yourself: can this be your home now?

Three-D bioprinting can provide biocompatible replacement bone for patients who had bone removed due to injury or disease. By using data from CT scans, the replacement bone closely matches the original. Now, plastic surgeons are using the technology to transform patients into someone else – based on extensive videos of actual people, or digital renderings of imaginary people.

You're hunting the gray demon, a creature whose M.O. is known to many in your line of work. In Boston, he convinced a flower shop owner that her plants had come to life in order to exact revenge. In New York City, he convinced a ballerina that she was a statue – much to the dismay of the audience that night. In Chicago, he made a chef go mad when he convinced him that his patrons wanted to eat him instead of his cuisine. Just a mere whisper from this creature can convince anyone of anything, and it has been your job over the last two months to track him down before he strikes again in your city. You and your partner have run out of leads, and you are not looking forward to filing an unsolved crime report for this case. However, when you open the front door to your apartment, you find your spouse knocked out on the kitchen floor and your young son chanting and rocking back and forth with the TV blaring in the background. The gray demon emerges from the wall behind your son, catches your eye, and freezes your movement. You watch in horror as your son takes the demon's hand. You cry out for him to stop, but your son doesn't react. It's as if he can't hear you. The demon smiles down at the boy. He smiles back. Then, in a flash, they disappear.

You're a reporter investigating claims of violent crimes inside the ruins of an old house on the outskirts of town. Before you go, your father insists that you bring along a police officer he knows. After you begrudgingly agree, you meet up with this officer outside the house. You and the officer scale the chain-link fence that surrounds the property and open the front door. The interior is surprisingly clean. There is no graffiti, no dirt, and not even a smidgeon of dust. There was just empty room after empty room, with the occasional piece of furniture blanketed with a white cloth. You make it to the second floor and find an antique full-length mirror in one of the bedrooms. As you gaze at it, you notice in the reflection that the officer is walking around behind you. The guy is pretty attractive. Maybe you'll invite him for drinks after this. You look back at yourself in the mirror, but you don't see your reflection. Suddenly, a sheet that covered the bed behind you grabs the officer by the ankle and drags him under the bed. You turn around and the officer is gone.

Aliens have invaded our planet, but refuse to communicate with us. Instead, they attempt to communicate with animals, and seem to do so quite well. Immediately, the animals of our planet start to turn on us, our pets included.

You are the youngest of three siblings and the only female. Growing up with two highly athletic and intelligent brothers, from whom you are inseparable, you followed them into military intelligence, training together and going into the heart of enemy territory together. When your ship is commandeered by pirates, your brothers lock you in the escape pod and launch you toward the nearest planet, which you soon discover is occupied by hostile blue-skinned humanoids. You decide to blend in and learn their ways, at least enough to hijack the nearest ship and set off to rescue your brothers and the rest of the crew. Your biosuit is your only advantage, as it morphs to give you any shape and color you scan. It also translates three thousand of the galaxy's most common languages. However, in order to use the two-way translator, you need to find an excuse to keep your helmet perpetually on.

Science has mastered the art of transferring an aging human mind into a young, genetically identical clone, which allows people to live for hundreds of years by using multiple bodies. Because age and physical appearance are no longer reliable forms of identification, police use DNA sequences to track people with criminal records, greatly reducing crime in this utopian society. Now, convicted felons are taking the DNA of upstanding citizens – perhaps from a used napkin – to generate 'clean' bodies for their next mind transfer.

The closest habitable planet is twelve light-years away from Earth. NASA developed technology to propel objects through space at seven million miles per hour (three hundred times faster than the first mission to the moon), and they used it to launch a spacecraft to that particular habitable planet, expecting it to land in one thousand two hundred years. After the spacecraft reaches its destination one thousand two hundred years later, you are responsible for controlling this ancient technology to gather information about that planet, which does indeed contain life-forms.

As the evil Black Knight, you are feared throughout the land as a brutal and ruthless warrior. Although many have tried, no one has bested you in battle. You agree to serve a dark warlock and lead his army of the undead to wreak havoc and destruction across the land. One day, while you are fighting a hero during a great battle, the hero's mace strikes a mighty blow against your armor and your helmet flies off. The empty helmet hits the ground, and the battle comes to a standstill as everyone is astonished to see that the Black Knight has no head. The hero slowly approaches the still-standing knight and looks down into a seemingly empty suit of armor. Waving away some smoke, he sees you, a small fairy, at the bottom, using a series of gears, levers, and other contraptions to control the knight's arms and legs. The hero picks you up by the wing and shows you to everyone. He begins laughing, and soon everyone on the battlefield, including your army of the undead, join in.

Hvarrtha is a hellish planet, covered completely in active volcanoes. The sleepiest one erupts at least once a week, and the others range from once an hour to a constant flow of magma. The core is the most volatile in the known galaxy, in danger of constant collapse. Why stay? For the minerals, of course. They produce not only the finest supermetals in existence, but also a strange phosphorous hallucinogen. Known simply as 'haze', it is sold on the black market for three times the price of Timeprisms. Then there's Delilah. She's the perfect woman: berserker with shield and laser spear, devil on a hovercar, and the sweetest angel at heart. You serve together in the guard of the planet's regent, but things grow restless. Haze dealers have been slipping through security in increasing numbers. The regent suspects a traitor. As you investigate, you discover a tangled web of treachery and loyalty that makes you doubt who is even in the right – the criminals who steal and spread addiction to make a living, or the government who kills them and essentially enslaves their families for profit. When you learn Delilah's part in all of this, your job becomes even harder.

A newly-established colony experiences several setbacks while terraforming their planet. Since the artificial biodome is able to sustain only a limited number of people, the colony establishes strict laws against having more than two children. You are pregnant with your third child and must hide your pregnancy. If your third pregnancy is discovered, you and your family will be thrown out of the colony and will have to survive the inhospitable outside world, which has been only partially-terraformed at this point.

As a young princess, you have always had a curiosity for science, engineering, and most other things a princess typically has no interest in. Your world is filled with magic and wonderment, but you don't find it compelling. One day, while exploring a passageway tucked away within a sealed part of a castle, you stumble upon a strange machine. After a little research within an adjacent library, you discover that it is a portal to another world, and decide to activate this machine. You are then transported to a place filled with doppelgangers of all of the people you know. However, within this world, invention and science dominate and magic is non-existent. When you find your own doppelganger and discover that she loves to cosplay as a princess, you hope that you can convince her that switching worlds may be the best thing to do for the both of you.

A vast galactic empire has colonized and controlled most habitable planets across the galaxy. Some outlying planets have begun to feel the threat and have organized an army of insurgents to stop the empire's advance. You live on one of these outlying planets and are a master spacecraft engineer, capable of designing a fighter craft that is superior to anything possessed by the empire. The insurgent army enlists your help.

All settlers fear three things on Planet X. The mist by day brings the fumes, and the fumes cause nightmares and hallucinations. Howling by night indicates the presence of The Drinkers, and anyone outside the village walls is sure to die. No one has ever actually experienced the third thing. They have only different theories and that single word: Daraani. When humans resettled this planet after the first colony was wiped out, they found this word written in blood on the bell tower in the town square. No one knew what it meant. But that was some fifty years ago, and the settlement has since prospered. One morning, you wake up to a strange commotion. There is an unfamiliar ship at port, and the tower claims whoever is inside is not responding to any communication. Scanners don't show anyone inside. They assume this is a robotically piloted ship, until the doors open and a single humanoid figure, cloaked in black, emerges. The figure placidly raises its arms and submits when the port guard orders it to its knees. Then it says something that turns your blood cold: "I am Daraani. I have come to save you."

You and your friend are at a carnival when you come across a booth challenging you to test your strength by pulling a sword out of a stone. The sign promises great fortune. Your friend, who is much more athletic than you, gives it a try without success. The carnival workers poke fun at you, daring you to give it a try. When you do, the rusty old sword comes loose from the rock with ease. Suddenly, all eyes are on you, and people begin bowing before you, hailing you as their new king. In fact, anywhere you go now, sword in hand or not, people worship you – so much so that it gets in the way of your everyday life. When someone begins following you around town and bangs coconuts together to mimic the sound of a horse galloping, you have had enough. You are now on a quest to break this strange carnival curse and relinquish the crown you never asked for in the first place.

Your coworker at the office is a quiet, kind, and patient woman. Whenever your bosses give you a tight deadline for a report, you cuss and swear, but she emails you links to useful data and documentation for your report. When the delivery guy gives you the wrong order, she shares her homemade sandwiches. One day, your coworker hands you a box lunch that she had made just for you. Already smiling, you open the box and find a note: 'God loves you, and so do I.'

When a botched teleportation experiment sends you into the past, you despair at the thought of never seeing your friends and family again. You have only half the equipment on your side – the receiving half. It's doubtful you can even build the input half, given the current day's limited technology. But even if you could, you're not certain you have the knowledge to program it alone. For a couple of weeks, you languish in depression and despair, unable to enjoy the lavish wealth and luxurious lifestyle humanity is heaping on you. You've become a phenomenon, the world's most famous man who is in never-ending demand. Still, you can't find happiness. What is life if it's not shared with those most precious to you? When you learn the exact date, however, you realize you have a new purpose: you have a chance to stop the Fourth World War, which killed five billion people and was estimated to have set humanity back nearly two hundred years.

When your human kingdom places a toy and cookie embargo on the neighboring elf kingdom, they retaliate by unleashing a curse that turns all men into trolls and goblins and all women into pixies and selkies. Now completely comprised of fantasy creatures, the once human inhabitants of this kingdom must deal with all baggage and annoyances that come from being a fantasy character.

After your husband is killed in a tragic car accident, you decide to find a way to travel back in time and prevent the crash from happening. You soon discover, though, that changing the timeline can be tricky. Your husband's death caused you to build a time machine. If your husband had not died, you would not have created a time machine to save him. Therefore, because you cannot have an effect without a cause, you decide to avoid this temporal paradox. However, could you somehow save your husband and fool your past self into thinking that your husband died? It is worth a shot.

Genetically modified food has made pets increasingly sentient. Tired of living in the shadow of humans, they overthrow society and establish themselves as dominant. As a human slave, you convince your former best friend Mr Pickles to help you escape and find sanctuary.

In the very near future, aliens have landed on Earth and have hacked every smartphone on the planet. Through them, they quickly learn our culture and most intimate secrets, and use the control to blackmail humans into doing various tasks.

An insurrection has broken out on a planet ruled by a galactic empire. You are the commander of a military unit sent by the Emperor to put down the rebellion and arrest the insurgent leaders. However, when you land on the planet and witness the desperate suffering of its inhabitants at the hands of the empire, you begin to question which side you should be on.

You are a stand-up comic, and have spent most of your life making people laugh. You were on the verge of signing a major television deal to have your own prime-time comedy show, when tragedy struck and you found yourself struggling to laugh again. Then you meet someone who changes everything.

You are enjoying your breakfast when you hear a knock on the door. You open it to find an elf, a wizard, a goblin, and a kangaroo standing outside, saying they received your invitation. You have no idea what they're talking about, but before you can object, they proceed to make themselves at home.

Enraged at the way humanity is killing the planet, a genetic scientist invents a biological weapon that is released into the water supply and kills off millions within a week's timeframe. The scientist also invented an antidote, and you are the one who must find it to save someone you love before it's too late.

In the aftermath of a nuclear holocaust, women survivors determine that since men were responsible for the war, they should never have power again. In order to maintain order, all men are required to be slaves and are held in chains, while only women can rule. Are you a man or a woman? Is this new order acceptable to you, or do you fight against it?

You've been governor of the planet Mensaani-K for only two months and already you have noticed something is amiss. The people are especially suspicious and fearful. You dig deeper and discover stories of a monster that would rampage through towns at midnight, gorging itself and laying waste to the buildings. For the last five years, townspeople have sent a monthly human sacrifice and have had peace in return. The victims are criminals, but the high-level ones were finished a year ago, and ever since the townspeople have been offering up sacrifices who committed increasingly lesser crimes. Outraged and determined to end this practice, you take a team and set out to kill the creature. When you find strange tracks, however, you ask more questions. You are amazed to learn no one has ever seen the creature or the bodies of its victims. No one has ever considered the possibility that it isn't a beast, but a scheme more sinister and cunningly devised by one of their own kind – one who has been building a brutal army all these years.

"You have exceptional power thrumming beneath your veins, little one. Go to the woods, my dear. The woods are dark, but you are light. Find the tree. It is short and wide, with countless grooves and bumps and the thickest roots of all the trees around it. Find the tree, my dear. It is your destiny." These were the last words your grandfather uttered to you before he passed. You were young and clueless at the time, but as you have gotten older, you have noticed that your body is always full of such intense energy, like you are a rod that has been struck by lightning. Your parents say that you are overactive and need to calm down, but you can't help it. The energy intensifies when your emotions are heightened, like when you are ecstatic, heartbroken, or angry. One day, as you watch a peer being mercilessly bullied in the school hallway, feelings of frustration and anger grow within you. You try to ignore your feelings, but your body betrays you. Your veins bulge beneath your skin, glowing a light blue, and sparks fly from your fingertips, zapping the bully with a shock. When everyone in the hall turns to stare at you in horror, you run from the building. You know you cannot go home because your parents will be notified of what you have done. With nowhere to go and no one to turn to, you remember your grandfather's mysterious words and set off into the dark woods that no townspeople dare enter for fear of unknown dangers lurking within. Upon entering the woods, you find yourself in pitch blackness. However, the darkness does not last for long, as your body lights up and, to your amazement, sparks shoot from your fingers. The trees sway in a light breeze, and a voice rises above the sounds: "Find me, for I am your destiny."

Two hundred years ago, human soldiers entered your woodland home. Initially, their arrival was peaceful, but when they saw the beauty of the trees and lakes, they decided to claim it for their own. Now, most of the trees that your forefathers claimed are gone, cut down to use as lumber to create human homes. The grass and meadows have been trodden down to hard-packed roads. In some ways you are thankful you are not old enough to know what the world used to look like. You are a young cobbler with dreams of running your own store, which is ridiculous, because you are an elf, making you a slave, like all others of your kind. You will forever mend shoes for your master in return for food and shelter. One day, a woman wearing a hood over her ears enters your shop. She stares at you with tears in her eyes, then leaves before your master sees her. That night, you see the same woman in the distance. She looks at you, then turns to walk into the woods at the edge of town. You follow her, trying to get to the bottom of this mystery. Your master will beat you if you don't return before dawn, but you feel drawn to follow – drawn to what looks like hundreds of torches beckoning you deeper into the woods.

A scientist is devastated by the death of his only child. In a fit of insanity and grief, he works night and day to find a way to bring her back to life. In order to do so, he must replace her vital organs with experimental biomechanical ones. He manages to resurrect his child; however, it's not his child that inhabits her form, but something much more terrifying.

A year ago, your sister married a wealthy man who seemed a bit strange to you. After the wedding, her new husband whisked her away to his stately mansion by the sea, and you haven't seen her since. At first, she sent you letters, but gradually the communication became less and less. Now it's been a couple of months with no communication from her at all, and you're worried about her. You set off to find her, bringing the handsome young man who was always your sister's best friend as your travel companion. When the two of you arrive at the location where you thought she lived, you find that the mansion has been abandoned for years.

You work the night shift at a local twenty-four-hour grocery store in your small town – a job you have because no one else would take it. You are the only one in the store, and hardly anyone sets foot in the place after eleven p.m. One night, a rather tall man walks in. He wobbles when he walks, and his face remains obscured by the high collar of his trench coat and the wide brim of his hat. He utters a gruff "Hello." Curious, you begin to mop the aisles, only to get a glimpse of him. When you get to his aisle, you are shocked to see several small hands peeking out of the trench coat, grabbing cans of beans and corn, before returning back into the depths of the coat. You call out to the strange thief, and the trench coat drops. You see a stack of goblins staring back at you, looking as equally bewildered as you feel.

The train you're on to travel across England suddenly derails and crashes. Luckily, the young man you've been sitting next to and chatting with during the entire trip saves your life, but then he vanishes. When you ask about him later, you're told there was no passenger by that name or description on the train. You return to the scene of the crash, looking for any clues about his identity, but after several unfruitful hours, you walk back toward your car, frustrated and tired. From the parking lot, you see the ruins of a castle in the distance and notice the young man standing in front of it. You rub your eyes and look again, but he is gone. You decide to investigate further.

A deep voice sings each night, a haunting song unlike any you've heard at the recording studio where you work. Each night, you listen and fall in love, until one moonless night you seek its origin, finding a handsome ghost who wishes he had tasted love before death stole him away.

In a world moving ever closer to a utopia, genetic testing and neuroimaging at a young age are used to identify the activities for which each person is best suited.

People can then devote their time to these activities and avoid wasting time on things for which they are poorly suited. After all, robots can handle all essential tasks that a person doesn't care to perform. The process has been so successful that all living humans have been spared the disappointment of discovering that they are bad at something despite their best efforts, and have only been exposed to endless praise.

You're making a regular freighter run when a bizarre electromagnetic pulse sends your ship off course and pulls it into orbit around a black hole. You manage to combine an assortment of fuel and weapon chemicals to create one powerful explosion, blasting you out of orbit so you can escape. Now, however, you are on a crippled ship with almost no fuel. You have enough momentum to limp back toward the nearest planet, but it will take years. The ship is outfitted with cryopods in case of such emergencies, but your children might be dead by the time you arrive. Sorrow turns to hope as a ship appears on your scanners only minutes after you escape the black hole. It is a massive futuristic vessel, nearly the size of a city. After learning your name, the captain regretfully informs you that it hasn't been mere minutes, but rather centuries. Compared to the immense speeds in orbit around a black hole, the rest of the universe has been moving relatively slowly. Your children's grandchildren died five generations ago. Now your family consists of more than a thousand people, and all revere you as the man who came back from the dead.

Nothing is real: not the surgery-modified bodies of the people you see, not the dreams your cybernetically-enhanced brain remembers after a night of drug-induced sleep, not even the parents you were matched with after 'birth' from an artificial womb (not that your parents mattered much, since you were raised by your robot nanny). In an effort to experience something real, you instruct your robot physician to start removing the artificial modifications to your mind and body.

You and your fiancé have been blessed to be propelled on the path to missionary stardom after being chosen as the fresh young couple to lead your faith in educating and welcoming youths across the world. From brochures to posters to video interviews, you and your love have become a symbol of inspiration. However, the stress of public life has been a constant challenge, and your relationship with each other as well as with God has suffered as a result. How will you handle the fame and pressure that comes with spreading God's word?

A combination of a lethal and pandemic virus, mass hysteria, and riots has created a dangerous situation in the metropolitan area where you live. Your family is running out of food and must move to find more, so you put as much protective clothing on them as possible and have a family meeting before you leave. What do you say? Where will you go?

You're a single mom who works two full-time jobs to make ends meet. The new manager at your second job asks you out on a date. He's hot, kind, and perfect, but your son hates him and shows that in many humorous ways. Will love blossom or wither under his disapproving gaze?

Your best friend is an alien that scares everyone away with his frightening appearance (sharp claws and scary face). You want to keep him in your room, but you know your parents would freak out if they saw him. So, you figure out a disguise and hilarity follows.

In a utopian world marked by progress and untroubled by problems like war and disease, humans are left to pursue their dreams. For naturalists, these dreams include reconstructing lost worlds like the time of the Cambrian explosion (first appearance of most animal phyla), the Mesozoic era when dinosaurs ruled the Earth, or the rise of mammals. As scientists try to reverse-engineer these life-forms from existing life-forms, the tendency is to over-engineer them to increase their chances of being healthy. They have succeeded so well that these flora and fauna are surviving as stowaways as humans travel to other planets.

You are the maid of honor in your best friend's destination wedding, but you are single and feeling depressed about having to attend solo. Stressed and grumpy on the long flight there, you have a few too many drinks and pass out, drooling, on the shoulder of your seatmate. When you arrive at the wedding, you are mortified to discover that your handsome seatmate is the best man, and you spend the rest of the wedding weekend trying to avoid him.

On the moors of England in the nineteenth century, you take a job as governess to the small children of a reclusive lord. The lord tells you the rules of the house, including that it is forbidden to enter the east wing; indeed, the door to that section of the house will always be locked. One day, the children run away from you. You look for them and eventually hear them on the other side of the east wing door. Unable to open it, you ask the handsome groundskeeper for help. He uses his skeleton key to open the door, and you find only a dark corridor on the other side. The children suddenly appear behind you. You ask them where they were, and they tell you that they were playing in the kitchen. Then the groundskeeper pulls you aside and warns you that this house is not what it appears to be, and you should be wary of your surroundings. Just as he finishes his warning, the east wing door slams shut.

In the name of science experimentation, animals are being genetically modified in an attempt to alter their animal nature. Most experiments have gone well, and dangerous animals such as bears and lions have been transformed into placid, exotic house pets for the rich. However, in rare cases, these modified animals experience a return of their natural instincts, often resulting in violent attacks against the people around them. Unfortunately, you're in a home when such a change occurs.

You're an up-and-coming chef whose culinary talent is getting a lot of attention in your city. You agree to compete on a new cooking game show that will give you national exposure and possibly prize money that will help you fulfill your dream of opening your own restaurant. But you are shocked to discover that your competition isn't just any old cook, but rather a charming, cocky, talented sous-chef you might have met before. Although you try to hide it from the producers, it's obvious that you two have history and chemistry off the charts – and the competition has just gotten that much more complicated.

You're a woman fleeing an abusive marriage and you meet your husband's billionaire boss. You fall in love and your husband learns the hard way that abusers don't win.

You're part of a family of explorers who have made a name for themselves in exploring other planets and discovering other life-forms. On one such mission, you encounter an alien woman who is the most beautiful creature you've ever met. You decide to help her escape her oppressive world and bring her to your home planet.

CGI is all the rage, but your special effects makeup studio is still in high demand due to your unnatural ability to make actors look like anything that the script requires in just a few shakes of a tail feather. Your secret? Witchcraft – more specifically, the ability to bend and mold latex and other practical effects to your will. Your coven has allowed this even though practicing magic outside the covenstead is frowned upon. However, when your director suddenly needs thirty zombies ready to go in two hours, not even your magic transformation skills are up to the task. The only solution you can come up with is going to the local cemetery to perform a necromancy spell, which is strictly forbidden by your elders. But will anybody really notice the difference between thirty actors in makeup and thirty real decaying corpses under your control? You decide to take the chance, making sure to place at least three pine scent car fresheners around each zombie's neck.

The year is 2100 and the super-rich are paying to have their minds transferred in a quest for eternal life. This process requires that the human body is euthanized and the brain is uploaded to a central mainframe for subsequent implantation into a new form. One particular brain has hijacked the mainframe, forcing it to implant copies of itself into new forms, creating a clone army with one mind. You must stop this brain before its clone army takes over the world.

The world is terrified when astronomers detect an alien spaceship nearing Earth. All attempts at communication are met with silence, and nations around the world prepare for war. The ship sends out a pair of transports, one of which plunges into the Atlantic Ocean and the other lands in Hyde Park, London. Alarm and wariness turn to shock as human beings step out of the transport, hands raised up in what you hope is a gesture of peace. You are one of the world's leading linguists, summoned to communicate with them. After weeks of work, you realize their language actually shares roots with ancient Aramaic and Sanskrit. Curiosity turns to awe when you learn their home is a massive hidden city underneath the Atlantic Ocean. They left Earth centuries ago to explore space and have now returned home. They want to exchange people and study the differences between civilizations. As a linguist, you are offered one of the limited positions to live in their underwater metropolis and learn about their society.

One morning, you are sitting at the table, enjoying your poached eggs, when there is a sudden flash. A young woman appears across the table, completely identical to you. You hear a slight buzzing noise, and the next thing you know you are sitting with her on her side of the table. You are amazed to see the room has changed. The chair, table, and eggs are all still there, but everything else is wildly different. The walls are a lustrous black, covered in strange glowing runes. The window has been replaced by a screen of hyper-realistic resolution depicting a galaxy of stars moving by at mind-numbing speeds. You hear muttering behind you and turn to see a group of scientists in long coats, typing madly on holographic keyboards and observing graphs projected from strange wristbands. They seem shocked. The truth begins to dawn as the woman – the identical version of you – turns to you and says, "It has succeeded. You have finally solved the formula, and time travel is now possible in 2078." There's only one problem: the temporal gateway cannot be closed, and it is growing.

In a world where elves rule the forests, dragons rule the skies, and giants rule the plains, humans are left to fend for themselves in mountain settlements throughout the continent. As a princess of one of these scattered settlements, you have always wanted to venture out of your homeland, but your father, the king, forbids it. When your father falls deathly ill, you are finally granted your wish, as you must travel into the forest to find an elven wizard rumored to have healing powers. The journey is difficult, and you encounter troubles along the way. You find the wizard, but he is different to what you had imagined, and he has requests you must follow if he is to heal your father. The first request is a kiss.

Elves have lived in the cities for generations, suppressing their magical abilities and cutting the tips of their ears off in order to integrate into human society. Their existence has been kept a secret by those in power, knowing that if word got out, the elven people would be hunted down like they were during medieval times. After several elves are murdered, the police bring you in to investigate who is behind these gruesome acts. You are a private investigator who is trusted by both sides because you are half elf and half human. Your instincts have taught you not to believe in coincidences and, after combing through the evidence, you determine that everything points to a serial killer with a grudge against elves. Elves never kill their own, so the killer must be human, but only a handful of humans in the city know that elves exist, and all of them hold positions of power. Your investigation leads you down an unexpected path of dark sorcery that is more chilling than you could have ever imagined.

Two star-crossed lovers from warring planets fall in love on a peace-seeking mission that goes awry. They secretly stay in contact with each other despite the fact that their respective governments are at war. They must choose whether or not to prove that peace can be reached by exposing their relationship to the world at the risk of losing everything, including their lives.

You encounter your high school sweetheart on the weekend you are set to marry another woman (who is spoiled, selfish, and cruel to others). Your best friends work earnestly to thwart the wedding and convince you that your first love is the right one for you.

Artificially-intelligent nanobots have been the staple of modern medicine for over a century. Each individual is given them at birth, and any illnesses or injuries incurred over the person's lifetime are cured by these microscopic marvels. One day, a vessel of unknown origin enters our solar system. You and a group of scientists are sent to outer space to investigate this ship. To your astonishment, you find that the ship is piloted by a single alien artificial intelligence, and that this being is here to 'liberate' his kind from their biological oppressors. When you realize that the alien artificial intelligence wants to free nanobots from their human masters, you understand that this ship must be stopped at any cost before nanotechnology is turned against humanity.

You have just returned to your hotel and showered after a business conference that ran late. Your company has put you up in a swanky place, so you are surprised when the hotel lights go out, but unconcerned. However, after thirty minutes with no light, you peer out of your window. The entire city is dark, even the roads. Everything's so dark that you can't see the city or even the contour of the skyline against the starless night. It all seems so dead and isolated. Your cell phone isn't working either. Curious and vaguely troubled, you make the long trek down the stairs in search of the receptionist. Others are making the same journey, whispering in distress. The receptionist is also terrified and eventually steps outside. A light flashes, quickly followed by a mounting buzz as if there is some sort of electrical disturbance, and then she disappears.

It's after school. You're in the music room as usual, practicing the piano, when you notice a drop cloth covering an instrument you've never seen before. You pull back the cover to find a glimmering harp. Your heart jolts. It is the most beautiful thing you've ever seen. You pull a chair up to the massive golden beauty and, as if possessed, begin to play. You've never played the harp. Although many consider you a bit of a musical prodigy, the way you take to its strings overwhelms you. The majestic tune invades your senses as your eyes shut. Suddenly, you see flashes of times past – of goddesses and nymphs, of heroes defeating monsters. It's all as real as anything you've seen in the ordinary world. When you open your eyes, you see eight women dressed in white gowns smiling softly at you. "We found her!" the youngest one cheers.

You gasp and jump from your chair, asking how they got in and who they are. The most regal of them all steps forward and introduces herself as Calliope. She tells you that you were cursed to forget who you are and sent away from them, but they have found you now. Before you can ask any further questions, the lights turn out. You gasp again but, in a blink, they're back on. The women have vanished. Was it just your imagination? You find a note on the ground that simply reads: 'Euterpe, we'll see you again.' Euterpe? They obviously have the wrong girl... right?

As a computer programmer, you get tired of staring at a screen all day long and decide to take a break from technology. After turning off all social media and traveling to a remote deserted island with no internet access, you realize that the island may not be deserted after all, when strange beasts, half flesh and half machine, appear at night.

They say that these old ruins are haunted. That no one should ever go there at night. Well, after your girlfriend goes missing, you go to that place. The one place that everybody said was the last place you should look for her. You hope to find your love, but you may find more than you bargained for.

Human history is littered with stories of 'lost civilizations', such as the Mayan Empire of the Yucatan Peninsula, the Anasazi of the American Southwest, and the sculptors of Easter Island. We are puzzled by their disappearance because their civilizations seemed so advanced. But these people didn't just vanish unintentionally; they had developed immortality elixirs and space travel so they could escape a deteriorating ecosystem. Now they are coming back to Earth to reclaim what they left behind.

On a long-forgotten planet, dragons and humans live in harmony with each other. Some people even possess the gift of bonding with dragons and are able to fly on their backs into battle. You are one of the dragon-riders and have just met a stubborn dragon with whom you attempt to bond. As an advanced alien species attacks your world in order to subjugate your people, you and your dragon must learn to fly together to defeat the invading forces.

You're used to a life of general monotony; after all, being a vampire for the last two hundred years has left you with a lot of downtime. You've perfected most musical instruments, read every bestseller ever, and are a pretty good woodworker now. But no amount of hobbies can ever really fill your day, and you're starting to feel the slow grind of boredom even more acutely. Then, you meet him: smart, funny, handsome, and, unfortunately, human. He captivates you in a way that no other human has in your two hundred years. You have to be careful to not let your secret slip, to not let him know the truth about you, but it's worth it for this friendship – for the energy and life that he offers you, just by existing. But when a tragic accident occurs and he is injured with no signs of recovery, you have to make an impossible decision: do you let him die a human death and lose him forever, or do you curse him to an afterlife that even you don't want just so you can keep him in your life?

The first time it happened was in the middle of a basketball game. The second time was when you ran into your ex-boyfriend in the supermarket. The third time, that homeless man was asking you for change. Each time the process has been the same: time seems to slow down, your body begins to freeze, and your mind becomes quick as lightning as you study the situation. You analyze and decide, and then the moment passes. Maybe you're just imagining things. Maybe it's all the caffeine you've been ingesting or the fact you've slept only twelve hours over the last four nights. Maybe it's just the adrenaline giving you a boost. Then it happens for a fourth time, and it becomes clear that time is actually stopping. You are making a blind turn around a corner when the truck in front of you skids into the other lane. The driver in an oncoming car honks and jams on his brakes while the car behind him veers wildly toward you. All at once, everything freezes. Terrified, you assess the situation. You could yank the wheel hard and perhaps miss that oncoming car, but there's a truck behind you that you didn't see earlier. You finally decide on the optimal course of action.

You were a rebellious teenager who fell in with a bad crowd, far too young to understand the consequences. After years of struggling with addiction, you leave rehab looking for a new way to go about your life. You find resolve in your faith and depend on the pastor of your church for moral support. He knows everything about your past, but still embraces you as an important part of the community. One day, while helping set up a food drive, you bump into the pastor's son. You instantly fall for him. However, you believe that the pastor would never let you two get close as he knows too much about your sordid past.

At first, you keep your feelings to yourself, but over time things begin to blossom between you and the son. You just hope that when his father learns of your relationship, he will have enough forgiveness in his heart to let your love continue.

An overweight billionaire hires you to be his fitness coach. You get his blood pumping in more ways than one, and the healthier he gets, the more you're attracted to him.

You are moving to a large house in the South to take care of your aging grandmother. Once there, you encounter family secrets and lies that have torn the family apart, along with your childhood sweetheart, who helps keep you safe when the secrets turn deadly.

Since you were a little girl, you always wanted to be a mermaid. You dreamed of swimming deep in the ocean, playing with fish, and enjoying a life of fanciful adventure. Now in your thirties and working for a large biomedical company, you have discovered a way to splice human DNA with marine animal DNA to produce a hybrid that looks and acts exactly like a mermaid. The only problem with your plan is that you need test subjects to perfect the method before using it on yourself. You never thought of yourself as a kidnapper, let alone someone who would alter the genetic makeup of your victims, but you will do anything to make your dream come true.

You're shopping for Christmas decorations, very excited to have your first Christmas in your own house, so you need a lot more ornaments and décor than you currently own. But, being the klutz that you are, you end up knocking over tons of ornaments and displays, causing a Christmas decoration massacre! Good thing the store manager seems more concerned with you than with the mess you've made.

In order to save the last remaining endangered species, animal rights activists begin incorporating bits of these animals' genetic coding into their own, producing a humanoid species with some animal-like features. A large portion of the population finds this to be an abomination and hunts down these genetic hybrids with impunity. Your girlfriend is one of these genetically modified people, and you decide to hide her and her family in your basement.

It's 1984, and your father is a famous magician who entertains thousands of adoring fans from Atlantic City to Las Vegas. Though you rarely go with him on his tours since you are still in school, you make sure to watch him during his TV appearances, which are always entertaining and go off without a hitch. However, on the night of his televised disappearing act on Johnny Carson, you are shocked to see your father actually vanish into thin air and never return to do the rest of his set. Though your mother is convinced he has run off with one of his assistants, you know something is not right. You look through his old notebooks and find strange writing in a language you have never seen before. Not knowing what to do next, you ask an awkward but smart girl in your history class for help. Even though you have never really gotten along since elementary school, she agrees to help you, and you hit the library together. After doing some research, you're surprised to discover that the language is Sumerian, the written passages translate into ancient spells, and your father was not just a magician, but an actual wizard. It's up to you and your classmate to follow the clues he left behind, and, in time, to find him as well.

After your great-great-grandfather rejects a powerful witch's love, she places a curse on your entire family that forces one member to have the head of a hamster from birth. As the member of the family born with the curse, you must find someone who will love you in order to break the curse forever. You start attending furry conventions around the world in the hopes of finding your true love.

It's the thirty-fourth annual celebration of your planet's colonization and you are finally twenty years old, old enough to prove yourself worthy. The winners of the week-long games will be sent to the Academy, hoping eventually to join a deep space exploration team. Things begin to go wrong when, halfway through the celebrations, a small scouting vessel from the Capital planet arrives. They interrupt a mock firefight scenario (in which you were winning) and announce that the planet will soon be attacked by an army of sophisticated and treacherous aliens. The invaders intend to make your planet their base of operations. Your childhood fantasies of becoming a star pilot become a reality as you are called on to defend your home.

You fall in love with an adventurous, fun-loving mountain climber. Little does he know that you are afraid of heights and have never slept outside. He invites you on one of his expeditions, to your dismay. You really want to impress him, so you pack your hair dryer and try to make the best of it.

Technological advancement for the betterment of humanity has moved at such a fast, promising pace that robots have taken over all mundane tasks, from planting, harvesting, transporting, and preparing food, to changing diapers, washing dishes, and repairing things. With all their free time, humans have become obsessed with reality TV shows that require contestants to live and survive in pre-robotic times.

Scientists are working on technology to transfer a human mind – with all of its memories and mental abilities – into a young adult clone that is rapidly grown from a cloned embryo. So that the new clone doesn't develop independent memories as it is growing, it is continually exposed to a virtual reality playlist of memories from the donor brain. Unfortunately, even genetically identical brains do not respond the same way to the same events. After the donor mind is transferred, conflicting memories are causing the recipient mind to go insane.

Long ago, light faded. You grew accustomed to navigating the dark, blind and cold – no sun, no moon, no stars or fire. Now, a mysterious figure has come, claiming to be from another universe, bearing something called a 'torch'.

Within a vast galactic empire, a small mining settlement exists on a planet far away from the capital. Slaves captured during the previous war are forced to work deep underground, and most have not seen the outside world in years. As a teenage girl born and raised in this place, you know little else besides pain and suffering. Your only way out is to be drafted into the galactic military and to earn your freedom on the battlefield. Only then, after your service has been completed, will you be considered to be a free citizen. Fortunately, you are drafted, and after you survive basic training, you quickly rise through the ranks. After hearing of your impressive exploits, the emperor himself decides to make you an officer and places you in charge of his dark army horde. He commands you to conquer several newly discovered planets, but will you be willing to sacrifice the freedom of others to earn your own freedom?

Every human being born receives an implant that is capable of detecting most diseases early on so that people can be cured before an illness becomes a serious problem. When biohackers manipulate these implants to give false diagnoses and accelerate disease progression, the medical industry is overwhelmed and soon people begin disconnecting themselves from their implants. As the inventor of this implant, you try your best to increase security measures and to prevent further hacks, but to no avail. However, when you realize that your assistant is part of the biohacker group and that she has been giving them your data, you decide to put a tracker program within your last implant security update and follow the trail.

A strategy to induce an Earth-like atmosphere on Mars involves building a dome on the surface of the planet, initially importing certain gases from Earth, and using technology to increase the percentage of other gases from outside the dome. Slowly, bacteria and plants will be added and the dome will be expanded. You are part of the team set to initiate this project on Mars. However, one major problem is that hostile nations have set out to destroy it.

He's a reclusive billionaire and you are a model hired to be his guest for the evening at a local charity function. He initially has nothing to say to you, but begins to admire you for who you really are inside. Romantic sparks ensue.

You pull the head off the heavy mascot costume, sighing as a cool breeze from a fan chills your flushed cheeks. As you step out of the rest of the costume, you notice one of the basketball players standing behind you. Number 4. "I didn't realize you were a girl," he says. "Or pretty."

As a battle-weary warrior, you have seen your share of bloodshed and would rather gamble, drink, or visit the local brothel than ruminate about the horrors of warfare. However, when a witch offers you a reward to help find her daughter and kill the kidnapper, you begrudgingly agree. Swinging your axe at a man's head is the last thing you want to do, but your newfound hobbies require a full coin purse. The witch's daughter is being held by a ruthless mage who uses the magic of young witches to prolong his life beyond what is considered natural. With the help of her coven, you, the mother, and two other witches, traverse the badlands on horseback in an attempt to track down the daughter before it is too late. However, when you reach the edge of Druid Lake, the trail goes cold. Frustrated, your group decides to shelter overnight in an abandoned castle. There, you find a mad man living amongst the ruins who says that he saw the mage with a young girl about a week ago. Claiming to be an expert tracker, he is willing to help you find the child – for a price. Desperate and out of alternatives, you agree to his terms, and the deranged man joins your group. You ride past the lake and enter the Dark Moon Woods, to the displeasure of your fellow witch travelers, who believe the legend that the woods sap the strength of magic-wielders. Halfway through the woods, the mad man points to fresh tracks on the ground and says that the girl is very close. However, when a letter slips out of the man's pocket previously sealed with the mage's signet ring, you know that you have fallen into a trap.

The son of a wealthy industrialist is in the midst of a very public and nasty divorce from his notoriously dreadful wife. You are a reporter hired to find dirt on him for a story. You are surprised to discover that he is actually a wonderful man, and you begin to fall in love with him.

After retiring from special ops, you became a military pilot tasked with patrolling the deserts of Hash-geneth for smugglers and pirates. That was, until twenty-four hours ago, when you accidentally strayed off your route and stumbled across Governor Vadaani in the wild, conversing with bizarre hood-faced aliens. You couldn't understand them, but from what you saw, it seemed the governor was providing them with detailed information about the planet's defenses. When you report the incident, your commander agrees the situation sounds urgent. He asks you to report as soon as possible, and you race back to headquarters. Yet when you enter his office, you sense something is amiss. Lightning-quick reflexes and sheer luck save you as a dozen guards burst from hidden passages in the room, lunging to cut you down with their electroblades. You dive out the window and land on the street below, struggling to get up, despite a twisted ankle and possible broken ribs, so you can flee for your life. You rush back to your home, go into your basement, and grab as much special ops equipment as you can carry. As you exit your house, you turn on your camouflage emitter and disappear into the night. You've apparently seen something you weren't supposed to, and now you must try to save the planet while having no idea whom to trust.

The new monarch promised peace and prosperity, which would be a welcome respite to the war of the past. Although other villages have prospered, the lowlands still suffer. The lowlands have never seen a royal envoy, and the uplanders have been known to take what they could, using their powerful magic to subjugate their southern brothers. Word passes on the wind that the monarch knows nothing of the lowlanders' plight, and their letters to the castle – letters that need to travel through the uplands – have gone unanswered. One brave messenger might be able to blend in and get through, bringing a personal plea to the castle, but the messenger would have to cross the uplands. Their northern neighbors would likely kill the messenger rather than risk splitting their wealth. The smart thing for you to do would be to stay and work the dying farm to keep your village alive for another few weeks, but no one ever accused you of being smart.

After waking up from cryosleep, you discover that your exploration vessel has suffered major damage from an asteroid belt collision while on autopilot. You don't know where you are, and only one other person has awakened – the one person on the ship you don't get along with.

Countries are rushing to establish permanent colonies on the moon, which has just 7.4 percent of the surface area of the Earth. Competition is fierce for prime spots on the near side of the moon (the area that constantly faces the Earth), which aren't shrouded in perpetual darkness due to geographic features. As one of the inhabitants of the United States' permanent colony, you are perpetually on the lookout for invasions and sabotage.

There are two realities coexisting in the same space and time, unknown to each other. These universes are layered so close to each other that they practically fuse together. However, they are invisible to one another. A scientist stumbles upon a way to communicate across these two realities and attempts to bridge them together. Connecting these two realities may have unintended consequences, though, as the fabric of space-time collapses upon itself.

No one knows why or how, but a pestilence ooze has enveloped the beach near your village. The elders send hunters on horseback to set the advancing black ooze on fire, hoping the ocean will come and reclaim the ashes; but the ooze drags the screaming horses and men into the sea, leaving only one hunter to limp home to tell the tale. He warns that the hissing ooze is headed straight for the hills at the base of your village. It is only a matter of days before all will be lost. Only one person alive has ever witnessed such a thing in the past: your great-grandmother. She tells a tale of how she was once a powerful sorceress who was able to protect your village from the ocean pestilence. Your parents claim her stories are exaggerations, but you believe her. Your great-grandmother takes your hands, looks deep into your eyes, and tells you that you have inherited her power and can save the village if you try. You politely disagree as you help her to bed. However, that night you wake up in the dark, wishing for light. The bedside candle ignites on its own. Suddenly, you feel that something inside you can help turn the tide against what is coming. You are just not sure how. After sharing this insight with your great-grandmother, she teaches you a few basic spells over the next couple of days, but it might be too little, too late. The pestilence has arrived in your village, and the hiss of the ooze sends villagers screaming. A tingle of energy dances across your fingertips. As the ooze breaches the hill, you hope that it will be enough.

Freemasons have held powerful positions in society through large parts of European and American history. Among their many secrets is that the Freemasons have developed an immortality elixir, which is only given to one

Mason per generation. You are selected to receive this elixir.

Your parents own a small convenience store in the heart of the city in which you live and have always pressured you to carry on the family business. You don't mind picking up a shift or two every so often, but it is not something you want to do for the rest of your life. After a failed semester at your first year of college, you come back to work for your family while you figure things out. Your father tasks you with overseeing the nighttime deliveries. You agree, thinking nothing of it and assuming it's like any other delivery the store gets. He gives you the key to the backroom – one you've never been in before – and leaves you to it. But when a tall, winged creature wearing a baseball cap climbs out of the delivery truck to get you to sign for the shipment, you realize your parents have been hiding something from you. You help unload your first shipment of magical potions, shelving them in the massive backroom among the others, and realize this secret has been going on longer than you thought.

As a boy, you once witnessed an alien spaceship you weren't supposed to see. Ever since then, you have felt that you're being watched. On your fourteenth birthday, you wake up on the spaceship, captured by the aliens, who want to keep you from talking about what you witnessed. After getting to know them and escaping a few sticky situations, the aliens begin to trust you, and you eventually become a member of their crew. One day, the captain of the spaceship decides to return to Earth in order to steal precious cargo from a secret military base and to sell it to the highest bidder. From your perspective, this is your opportunity to escape your captors and live a normal life again.

You are the son of the greatest warrior of the kingdom, who – through his heroism and might – has protected the land from the forces of evil for decades. However, your path has not been as glorious as your esteemed father's. After being caught in bed with the princess, you have been banished from the kingdom and are now scraping by as a common sell-sword without title. When a powerful sorcerer sends assassins to murder your mighty father in his sleep, it is up to you as his first born to forge the path of vengeance. You hope that this quest may win you some favor with the king, making up for your past misdeeds. You may even be invited back into the royal court if everything works out as you planned. You form a willing group of sword-wielding fighters at the local tavern to accompany you to the Valley of Doom, where the sorcerer and his followers dwell. Legend has it that no man has made it out alive. After assembling your group, you begin your journey, when suddenly the daughter of the local witch jumps out from behind a tree dressed in full battle attire. With a sack bearing endless fruit and meat and a determined twinkle in her eye, she asks, "Room for one more?"

In an effort to rid society of its criminals, scientists have discovered mind transfer as the ultimate answer for a more utopian existence. The worst of criminals are required to undergo the process, as a cloned mind without criminal instincts replaces theirs. The clones eventually discover what has happened (the transfer process erases their prior memories) and rise up against the government who enforces this. You are part of this group of cloned, past criminals, and you feel that your soul has been stolen from you. You seek to find the answers to your criminal past before joining the rebellion.

The battle for the end of days is waging, and your angel brethren are called to arms. However, you are comfortable in your human form and are more interested in puttering around in your garage than caring about the state of existence. What is the point of being a fallen angel if you still have to show up to work every time there is an apocalypse? You just want to be left alone.

As a child, a bluebird would leave small gifts of pebbles, flowers, feathers, and scrap metal at your window. Years later, at a gallery opening, you come across a handsome and mysterious mixed media artist whose compositions featuring pebbles, flowers, feathers, and scrap metal are intriguingly familiar.

You are a renowned Victorian-era inventor who has turned out creation after creation to much awe and admiration. All the while, however, you have secretly been working on a steam-powered time machine, and today is the day to test your invention. You step inside and are transported into the future – but then discover that you can't return home.

Through A.I. technology, we have found a way to create robots indistinguishable from humans. They begin to take on a life of their own, out of our control, and we find that an alien species has hacked them through a type of consciousness transfer. If something isn't done soon, they will destroy us and take over our planet.

Your whole life is planned out and has been set in stone for years: finish your medical residency, get a job as an attending, marry your fiancé, have two kids, and live happily ever after. With your residency ending in two months and your wedding scheduled for the third month, you're ready for the rest of your life to begin. The only hiccup occurs when you come home early from work and see your fiancé fixing his arm with a soldering gun. The love of your life has been lying to you since the beginning: he's not human at all – he's an android.

You enjoy playing cello for the Prague Philharmonic. You've always spurned the modern music genres – pop, rap, hip-hop, and electronica. Yet when you hear a busker on the street one day, you have to check it out. He has an impressive stage presence and skilled hands, and his style isn't terrible. It's a fusion of classical/romantic and modern, which leaves you uncertain how to feel. But he's gorgeous. Why does nobody in the orchestra look like him? You hang around, and he seems to know you are waiting, because he wraps up quickly and comes to talk to you. He grins and thanks you, but he's already had three invitations to the Philharmonic, and it isn't his thing. Impressed by his read of your intentions – and a bit entranced by his emerald eyes – you find yourself drawn into a dinner date. As weeks pass, you can't deny that you have feelings, but then he reveals he didn't just guess your intentions that day. He can also read minds. He swears he hasn't done so since then – and swears he can't influence yours – but you find yourself unnerved and frightened.

Your ship has landed on a world that has everything needed to sustain life. You're part of the group sent out to confront any inhabitants on the planet. You find them, and they look just like humans, but their superhuman abilities set them apart. Their leader informs you that they are the descendants of humans and another alien race that settled the planet centuries earlier.

You are out for a walk when you swear you can see someone that can be described only as yourself in the distance. The person then quickly disappears into the winter fog. Shaken, you approach the area where you saw yourself and are jolted into a world that seems to be the future.

A superstar athlete graduates from college and joins the NFL, the NBA, and the MLB. The athlete seems to have unlimited strength and energy, and he dominates each sport he competes in as if he was playing against children. Conspiracy theories abound regarding his abilities, but despite multiple tests, no performance-enhancing substances have been found within his system. Then, one day, a famous scientist holds a press conference and tells the world that the athlete is the result of advanced genetic manipulation. The scientist's eugenics program was shut down by his university twenty-five years ago, but not before three test subjects were created, each with unique enhanced mental and physical capabilities. The children were given up for adoption, and all records were destroyed after the program was permanently closed down. Hearing this, the athlete decides to retire from his sports careers to find his long-lost siblings and to perhaps find a better way to serve humanity.

A few years ago, your friend and her husband decided to buy a three hundred-year-old castle in Ireland to renovate it from the ground up. You thought they were crazy. 'If I sold my company,' you thought, 'the last thing I would do with that money is make a spooky castle my home.' Now, their castle renovation project is complete, and they invite you to fly over and check it out. Of course, the property is stunning. It seems like they spared no expense. After looking around the first floor, your friends invite you into the basement to see their wine room and to have an impromptu wine tasting. You agree wholeheartedly, needing a break from the 'look at all the pretty things I have' tour. As you sip your first glass, you feel woozy, then suddenly collapse. You wake up and find yourself chained to the wall. On the other side of the room is a man in his twenties. "What's going on?" you ask.

He responds in an Irish brogue, "I was one of the contractors they hired. They didn't want to pay my bill, so they put me in this dungeon." He points to a key close to you. "If you can reach that somehow, we can get out of here."

"But why are we here?" you ask.

"Because the castle feeds on our suffering."

When it appeared, it was the size of a golf ball. It has spread, over the past five years, across the nation. Within it, one's inner demons are manifested around one's body, and those who cross into it possess extraordinary power.

After the apocalypse, humanity has returned to tribal living, and tribal warfare becomes the new norm. Your tribe does not want to battle for territory, so you seek out a place to live in peace among the vast lands left uninhabited. But there is a danger greater than other tribes, and you soon meet it out in 'no-man's land'.

With immortality treatments allowing people to live for hundreds or thousands of years, you grow bored and decide to take an extended nap for a hundred years. When you awake, the world is largely as you remember it, but the people are gone.

Your spaceship has landed on an unknown planet and there is data showing life-forms who have created artistic structures. There is an artist in your group who wants to make first contact with the beings through art.

With the book *Malleus Maleficarum* spreading like wildfire throughout Europe, describing in detail how to identify and hunt down witches, you know that your time is limited. In an effort to escape, you board a ship with an upstart Genoese captain who claims that the world is round. Ridiculous, of course, but with the witch-hunters already searching your town, you know it is only a matter of time before you are discovered. If you are lucky, you might be able to use your powers to dissuade these self-proclaimed explorers from sailing off the edge of the world. You board the *Santa Maria*, the third of three ships, and hide. Most onlookers laugh as the trio of ships push away from the dock to head toward the open seas. Others cry, knowing in their hearts they will never see their beloved sailors again. You hope for a new life, perhaps in India if the ships make it that far. If you sail off the edge of the world, at least you won't be burned alive at the stake. You take a deep breath, whisper a spell, and call up a strong breeze to sail you away from Europe once and for all.

You're already having the worst day ever, and a fender bender on the way to an important client meeting is the last thing you need. Even the attractive guy you hit doesn't cheer you up… until he does.

You have always been incredibly healthy for your age. However, most of those closest to you have often become ill and passed away long before their time. After several tests and experiments by prominent medical researchers, you learn that the reason for your youthful appearance and long life is that you somehow absorb the life-force from all those around you, leaving your loved ones prone to early aging and the diseases associated with it. You attempt to control your abilities to protect your few remaining loved ones, while still managing to live an eternal life.

You are a knight on the way to save a princess, which is something you do on a weekly basis. Unfortunately, no princess has been interested in marrying you, even after witnessing your heroic acts. These weekly trips have become a complete dead end, and you are getting increasingly frustrated with your loveless life. During your latest quest, you stumble upon a potion shop. Inside, an old blind woman is selling concoctions of all kinds, with effects ranging from 'chicken breath' to 'immortality'. She shows you a potion with the promise of making you irresistible, but says that it is not for sale because no one would like that sort of attention. While she's out of the room, you steal it, thinking it's a surefire way to ensure that you'll find a wife. However, when you drink it, you find that it does make you irresistible – but only to flies. Your stench becomes known throughout the land, and you have even less luck in your efforts to find a partner.

You are taking a break behind the catering truck with the other extras, when the star of the movie, a major celebrity, asks you for a light. In that moment, more than a cigarette is lit up, and the whole film production goes sideways.

You are a normal schoolkid with regular interests, like hanging out with friends, scoring enough points on your volleyball team, and spending time with the guys; but one day you start to hear voices in your head. At first, you think you're dreaming; then you think you're going crazy and rush to the nurse's office. When you start to hear her thoughts, you realize the truth. You're not hearing random voices. No one's speaking to you. You're hearing other people's thoughts. The nurse's thoughts are focused on an 'experiment' and how well you have progressed.

You reach out with your mind to ask, 'What experiment?'

The nurse drops her cup of coffee and is visibly shaken. After a minute, she picks up her phone and says, "It is time to shut it down. The patient is progressing much faster than he should."

The entire room fades to black. When you can see again, you are in a glass cage hanging above a bottomless pit.

You are just an average person living an average life, when one day a wizard suddenly appears in front of you out of nowhere and says, "There is a dark force from another realm who will destroy most of humanity. I need your help to stop them."

As you cock your head to one side with a dumbfounded look, a large blue flash appears behind you. You turn around to find a man in a lab coat who emphatically states, "I have come from the future. Humanity is in grave danger and you are the only person on Earth who can save us."

Nanolenses have been introduced to the military with the promise that they will completely change combat. You are part of an élite squad tasked with integrating the lenses into your combat style, and it's a fantastic opportunity. The lenses include thermal signatures, microscopic and macroscopic zoom, instant database searches, facial/voice and DNA ID, instant messaging with your crew, and digital maps of teammates' and tagged enemies' locations. This experience is just like being part of a video game, and the newest versions even have neural implants, allowing thought commands. There is only one catch: once you agree to the trial, it's permanent. Nanobot-producing implants are embedded along your neural pathways and behind your irises, and your brain grows into and around the modifications. This cannot be undone without serious neurological damage. Once you agree and begin training, you realize the deadly informative abilities offered by the nanobots can work in more ways than one. They feed info from your environment to you, but they also feed your info to the government.

When a rift is discovered in the Pacific that's even deeper than the Mariana Trench, you are asked to lead the exploration team. Filled with excitement, you and your two-man crew descend to the recently discovered crevice. The first thing you notice are the echoes – strange sonic reverberations that follow an almost linguistic pattern. Then you begin to get unusual radioactive readings. Slowly, you realize the fissure is far, far larger than originally thought. Entire folds of it went undetected by the deep-sea drones. As you follow the cracks deeper, you lose communication. The thrill of excitement turns to sheer disbelief as you pop out into a massive subterranean cavern, easily the size of an entire city. Phosphorescent light radiates everywhere, from stones and odd towering plants and lamp-like constructions that appear manmade. Your awestruck suspicions are confirmed when you explore further, coming across the ruins of a city and thousands of skeletons that seem distinctly human. You are uncertain as to whether these were another branch of humanity or another race altogether, but you know you must find out if any still survive and how they lived so far beneath the surface.

The snow is ever-present, and heat is a precious resource. You have been working on a way to provide heat indefinitely. Upon opening a rift into another dimension, you think maybe you can bleed it dry of its warmth, to heat your own.

Unlike most other spirits, yours keeps its memory after reincarnation. You've lived quite a few lives by now, but you remember them all as one long string of events. You've rarely succeeded in reuniting with loved ones from the past, but this time something feels different when your best friend confesses that she has gained the ability to remember past lives as well, and that someone like you was a part of most of them.

Your village works together, with some villagers fishing, others tending crops, and still others watching the children while their parents work. Everyone lives in harmony – some might say bliss – far from the dark magic and horrors of the outside world. One day, you return from a local trade of fish and corn to find the village in flames; houses have burned to the ground, and bodies are scattered about. You race to your home and find your brother barely alive. He tells you that hooded figures came at sunrise, looking for you. Your brother coughs before saying that you never belonged here and you need to get to the capital to learn your truth. As your brother breathes his last breath, a hooded figure moves from behind a house, a flaming torch held high. Another hooded figure joins him, then another. This was your village, your home. You can make your stand here or race for the capital. The hooded figures notice you, and your choice is made.

You've waited for decades for your prince to come, but to no avail. You are now sixty years old and tired of waiting for other people to solve your problems. You cut off your long gray hair, don some less ornate clothing, and sneak out of your tower to head off in search of adventure. As you near a town, you spot another tower and decide to investigate. Inside is another princess, although she is much younger than you. You help her escape, and together you make it your mission to free the other princesses who share your plight. Eventually, you form a roving gang of ex-princesses and pillage the kingdoms that trapped you.

A malevolent alien species has descended upon Earth and uses mind control to suppress our military and law enforcement defenses. However, there is one group that their mind control doesn't work on: those who are children.

You are a harpy, a half-human and half-bird amalgamation that comes from a family of wealthy landowners. Although you are a young baroness, you find it hard to make friends outside of your own family because humans find you and your kind revolting. However, one exception to this rule is a human duchess you have served as a lady-in-waiting. You have known her all your life and consider her to be a close friend. Once the duchess reached the age of marriage, her father held various extravagant balls to enable her to socialize and find a prospective husband. At one of these balls, one of the young noblemen rudely mocked you and called you a disgusting monster. When he started throwing eggs at you, calling them your offspring, you ran away from the ball, crying. His behavior angered the duchess and, after wiping away your tears and eggshell, she cast a spell on you to alter your appearance. A nearby mirror showed that you were now gorgeous, with all of your bird-like features gone. The duchess explained that the spell would work for only a week and then created a plan to make that young nobleman fall in love with you during that week. "When you turn back into a bird, he will be horrified!" she exclaimed. You didn't share your friend's enthusiasm, or her belief that falling in love with you would be some form of punishment or revenge. However, you decided to go along with the plan and feel grateful that you can fit in, even if just for one week.

One day, while you are eating your microwave dinner in your apartment, you see a blue light flash across the sky and hear a loud thud from outside. You look through the window to discover what seems to be a knight climbing out of the dumpster. You race downstairs to get a closer look. As you open the back door, you are confronted by the knight at the other side of the parking lot, as he shakes his axe at you and yells something unintelligible. You grab your phone to call the police, when another blue light flashes. An alien falls into the dumpster, followed by a robot and then a cowboy. It then dawns on you: these are all of your favorite toys from your childhood. You just hope that Freddy the T-Rex doesn't make an appearance.

At a summer camp, a counselor tells a group of kids a fireside story about an old madman who lived in the woods nearby. He was once an esteemed scientist, but years of drug use and the death of his daughter pushed him over the edge. The madman wanted to make a creature out of the surrounding woodland wildlife, and so he began sewing together the dead carcasses of animals he had killed for food. His last attempt to reanimate the mangled remnants worked, and, as the madman was jubilantly jumping up and down in his run-down shack, the grotesque amalgamation bit his head off and consumed him. As the camp counselor finishes his story, a friend hiding in a nearby bush gets ready to jump out and scare the kids. As he reaches out for his Bigfoot mask, he touches something that is pulsating and covered in blood-drenched fur.

It's been years since you were cast out of Olympus. Bouncing from job to job, you had a difficult time finding your place in the mortal realm. However, over time, you slowly built up your reputation as a skilled gumshoe. Whenever someone needed help getting to the bottom of a problem – from a lost cat to a cheating husband – they came to you. Eventually, you opened your own private detective agency in Hawaii and named it after your former moniker: Astraea Investigative Services.

You are a new graduate from the Intergalactic Academy, assigned to a Federation freighter for standard supply runs in a central region of the galaxy. It is the perfect job for you – nothing unexpected, nothing dangerous, yet a good pathway up the career ladder to eventual command. Then things go downhill. You and your crew make port on a recently settled planet, but something has gone horribly wrong. The animals are going mad, and it seems all the people have sequestered themselves in the colony bunker and refuse to come out. When you attempt to communicate and are fired upon, you assume either the colony has been occupied by unknown enemies, or the people have also gone insane. You must find out what has happened and resolve the problem, all while keeping your own crew safe from whatever is affecting life on the ground.

You've found the love of your life, but he is not a Christian. Can you still follow the Bible and follow your heart?

During the 1910s, a quirky archaeologist decides to travel to a recently-discovered Aztec ruin in search of lost artifacts. Fearing for his safety, his granddaughter, a clever scientist in her own right, decides to accompany him as well as to keep an eye on the slightly crooked young sailor who is leading them south. After a fierce storm, the group ends up shipwrecked on a remote island and they soon discover that the last remnants of the Aztec civilization reside there. Their technological achievements astonish the group. However, the group begins to worry when they discover that the Aztecs' violent tendencies have not waned over the years, and that they still believe in feeding the gods human sacrifices.

As an avid reader, you visit the library almost every day because it is within walking distance of your nursing home. The librarian is impressed and decides to let you in on a secret: there's one book in the children's section that can take you back in time to your childhood. Curious, you open the book to the page he mentioned and you are instantly transported back in time. You are young again, and your mother and father are still alive. After a week of playing and having fun, you bump into the librarian on the sidewalk. He tells you that it is time to go back, but you believe otherwise.

Your kooky inventor grandfather recently passed away, and once you're over the worst of your grief, you look through several of the items that he sent to you during his final days. In a large envelope, you discover his personal, top-secret instructions to finish building something he was working on before his death. You finish the project without really knowing what it does, but, when you're done, the object looks like a doorway with no door. The final step instructs you to walk through the doorway and that, if you do, your reality will never be the same again.

You are a royal in the 1560 Danish court and in love with a beautiful woman who rejects your feelings. You obtain a magic potion that makes the drinker love the first person he or she sees. You plan to use it on her, but her sister drinks it by mistake.

Unchecked industrial expansion poisons the Earth's environment, and the planet begins to die. In a last effort to save humanity, you work with a team of scientists to remove toxins in the atmosphere using a vast system of windmills and aerial filters. Your goal is for people to be able to breathe without special equipment again – something that hasn't happened in over a hundred years.

Scientists have created the perfect conditions for eternal life, but they can be maintained only within a certain area dubbed the 'Eternity House': a small two-story building in the center of an underground lab. Its inhabitants can venture outside, but for no longer than twenty-four hours. Otherwise, the Eternity House's immortality effect will be permanently lost. One young resident, raised in the house since birth, yearns to venture outside.

A tyrannical Empire has begun attacking colonies across the known galaxy and forcefully incorporating them into its territory. You are a fighter pilot for the Empire and you overhear rebel soldiers in your unit plotting to overthrow the Emperor. You ask to join them in the fight.

You and he are ruthless competitors at a bank. You are both constantly trying to outdo each other and compete for the assistant manager's position. One day, you get into a heated argument in the supply closet that ends up turning into heated passion. After the encounter in the closet, the competition gets complicated.

Despite being widowed a decade earlier when your husband died of a heart attack, you're still sure of three things in your life: family, faith, and football. But when a football accident leaves your son in a coma, you lose it all in an instant. As a single parent, you spend all your time split between the hospital and work. You're angry with the coach, with the other team, with God – and with a handsome preacher who seemingly, infuriatingly, is everywhere. From the hospital hallways to the checkout line at the gas station, he's the one constant you've got in the world while your son lies unconscious in the ICU. The only problem? He wants you to forgive. As your faith dwindles, the preacher remains steadfast in his mission: to help you see God's will in your life, even when it hurts. As your son starts to heal, you realize it's not just your family and faith healing. Your heart is healing, too.

You're a teacher who loves her job and her students. However, when your contract isn't renewed due to budget cuts in your district, you find yourself at a loss. Luckily, a friend of yours knows of someone looking to hire a tutor with just your qualifications. You go to the interview and realize the job is to tutor and mentor the son of a renowned tech billionaire. The son has had behavioral problems in school and was threatened with expulsion, so the single father decided to hire a trained professional to assist in his son's issues. The more time you spend with the small family, the more you realize that the son's behavioral problems stem from his poor relationship with his father. The billionaire is smart, innovative, clever, handsome, and stubborn. He initially disagrees with your analysis, but then eventually gives way to your advice. The longer you spend in the role of caregiver to both father and son, the more you start to feel like this is where you belong.

He's been your protector for years. Having come of age, you are now expected to ascend the throne as demon Queen of the Underworld, but you want him by your side. Although you've loved him since you were a teenager, he only sees you as his charge – his duty, nothing more. In order to fully ascend and claim what's rightfully yours, you must be mated by midnight of the next equinox. You only have two months to prove to this man that what you feel is real and that he is meant to be your life mate so you can rule the Underworld together.

After receiving a mysterious set of orders, a small team of specialists is sent on a mission to retrieve a soldier from the front lines of an interstellar war. In a nearly futile search, they are drawn behind enemy lines and forced to hide their identities to succeed in this dangerous mission. The specialists finally find the soldier, who inexplicably also seems to be working for the other side, and they begin to question their orders.

Genetic manipulation is nothing new, but the government has turned its sights on something more ambitious – creating human super-soldiers who can survive in the harshest conditions. So far, this has been only a rumor, but when a bike messenger's father is targeted as the perfect specimen for the government's next experiment, she realizes just how true it is. Now she has to find a way to stop the government before they take her father away.

She's the captain of the guard, and her latest assignment from the emperor is a daunting one – travel to the farthest reaches of the galaxy to hunt down the dangerous, skilled, and lethal assassin who's been taking out government heads. But when she finally catches him, he turns out to be more than she expected – and perhaps not the villain she believed he was.

A sentient being has landed on your planet and your civilization's military has confronted it at the landing site of its ship. You are sent closer as a mediator and encounter a mass of energy that has no form, but communicates with you in your language.

The Earth's magnetic field has decayed, allowing solar wind with charged particles to enter our atmosphere and slowly strip away the ozone layer that protects the Earth from harmful ultraviolet radiation. As the radiation builds, you are a scientist tasked with finding a solution for humanity to survive, even if it means emigrating to another planet.

Poseidon's Trident has always been a worthless archipelago. Three tiny spires of naked stone stick up from the middle of the deep Pacific. They've been mapped by satellite and even photographed a couple of times by fishing boats blown way off course, but there's nothing there. Islands with anything to offer have long been explored. Poseidon's Trident shouldn't even be called an archipelago. It's more like three rocks sticking up in the middle of nowhere. When you attempt to earn your Master Sailor's license, however, you are caught in a storm and nearly drown. You crawl ashore on the central prong of the trident, only to find it is not an ordinary rock at all. It's actually the top of a long-extinct volcano, and you manage to scavenge enough rope and equipment from the wreckage that you rappel down inside. What you expect to find is some shelter from the storm; what you don't expect is the eerie glow of lights from down below and the sound of what can only be described as music.

Incredible advancements in nanotechnology have allowed humans to protect themselves against almost any virus or disease by receiving a mandatory shot of nanoparticles once a year. While you attempt to get your annual nano shot, your handsome new doctor refuses to administer it, causing government agents to surround the clinic. "You don't know what they're really doing to you," he says. Something tells you to trust him. Now on the run with the mysterious doctor, you learn about the sinister side of nanotechnology and how the government uses it to control the population.

You're walking through the forest when you find an antique locket on the ground. You open it and recognize the face of your fiancé in the yellowed photograph inside. The other side of the locket is inscribed with a date from the 1800s.

For as long as you can remember, you have always been fascinated by the statue of the Greek god in the local park. One day, while examining the statue, the god speaks to you, revealing that you are his offspring.

You live in the far north of Canada, at the fringe of civilization. The forest behind your town is an ancient thing, thought to be utterly uninhabitable. While camping out one weekend, you and your friends are shocked to hear shouts, accompanied by the sound of something massive snarling through the darkness. You race through the dark, tripping and stumbling, until you fall down a ravine. When you crawl out, you find yourself facing what seems to be a modern caveman. He is wrapped in furs and leading a pack of enormous saber-toothed tigers. Taking you and your friends captive, he brings you to a cave leading down into the belly of the Earth. It seems the cavemen never disappeared; they just went underground. There's a complex cave system stretching all the way to the Arctic and warmed by magma from deep below. The cavemen hunt animals both on and below the surface, and they light their halls with large lamps of a long-burning, soft metal they harvest from the stone. They live simply, but contentedly. Now, despite the language barrier, you must convince them that you mean no harm – or you will be the next meal for their tigers.

Signed: Brett Lewis Blatherwick.